T0060831

THE WONDER OF
TERRA

THE WONDER OF
TERRA

THOMAS W. BALDERSTON

TATE PUBLISHING
AND ENTERPRISES, LLC

The Wonder of Terra
Copyright © 2015 by Thomas W. Balderston. All rights reserved.

No part of this publication may be reproduced, stored in a retrieval system or transmitted in any way by any means, electronic, mechanical, photocopy, recording or otherwise without the prior permission of the author except as provided by USA copyright law.

This novel is a work of fiction. Names, descriptions, entities, and incidents included in the story are products of the author's imagination. Any resemblance to actual persons, events, and entities is entirely coincidental.

The opinions expressed by the author are not necessarily those of Tate Publishing, LLC.

Published by Tate Publishing & Enterprises, LLC
127 E. Trade Center Terrace | Mustang, Oklahoma 73064 USA
1.888.361.9473 | www.tatepublishing.com

Tate Publishing is committed to excellence in the publishing industry. The company reflects the philosophy established by the founders, based on Psalm 68:11,
"The Lord gave the word and great was the company of those who published it."

Book design copyright © 2015 by Tate Publishing, LLC. All rights reserved.
Cover design by Carlo Nino Suico
Interior design by Manolito Bastasa

Published in the United States of America
ISBN: 978-1-63367-289-5
Fiction/Alternative History
14.10.23

This book, as with all I write, is dedicated to my wife, our children, in-laws, grandchildren, my brother and his wife, and extended family. May they all find through my faith a renewed or increased conviction in their own Christian belief. To my friends who have walked before me, with me, and past me, thank you, and may you stay on your path and continue to guide and inspire others as well as me. To everyone, who reads this book, thank you for considering my work, but more importantly, if not a believer, may you become a fellow believer and find inspiration in the Word. If you do believe, thank you for your indulgence, and bless you; and if you find only a small nugget from this book that can make the truth better understood or provide some clarity, a new idea, or approach, praise God. May God find your center and may you become a God-centered Christian. My hopes and prayers are with mankind.

Acknowledgments

Writing this piece has been fun, in all honesty I have enjoyed every moment. It was a learning experience. Many thanks are needed. I have already thanked those writers who provided inspiration through their own works to enlighten mankind to God's presence.

To Sue Brehm for aiding in the review and multiple times copying and binding drafts for reading by friends and family, a special thanks.

To my wife, Dee, for being supportive throughout, even reading with a confused look at times at my scientific jargon but helping prepare a message.

To our ministers and pastors, with a special thanks to Buz McNutt, the pastor at First Baptist of Boynton Beach, Boynton Beach, Florida, for the lunches we shared, the discussions we have had (and I hope continue) and for his explanations of subjects understood by me in a superficial fashion to which he was able to add depth and clarity.

To the men in my Men's Bible Study for continuing to stick with their commitment to weekly meetings and discussions of topics enhancing their faith and their personal relationships with the Lord. This has been and will continue to be a journey, a rewarding journey along a faith-based path. With your continued support and love may it endure until God calls.

To our children and grandchildren may they discover the depth of the faith of their parents and grandparents and renew or simply further stimulate their own faith. Melisa, Amanda, Kristin, Tommy, Madison, Carter, Mia, William, Owen, Jake, Brooks, Anne Lane, Alexander, and Abigal-Louise, I dedicate this work. A special thanks to Madison, who took a student approach to the story, asked good questions and showed a level of intellect and understanding that is what truly excites a grandparent. Then too children through marriage, Tim, Bryan, Mike and Marilyn, may you all realize that life is made fuller by your faith in the Lord.

To those that read this short story, thank you, may it open your eyes in a way that causes you to look more deeply into what you believe. Follow the evidence with an objective view, a mind unencumbered in any way, and see clearly your own pathway to the truth. Let your doubts be couched as questions and seek the answers, considering differences and allowing for change in your current way of thinking, if indeed that is what is called for. Let you mind, your heart, and your soul see and seek God.

Contents

Now, But Then, What Really Happened?

"How did it end?"

"Why were we chosen?"

"Are we deserving of this paradise?"

As two strolled a street lined with life-giving and sustaining trees, a clear blue sky above, a conversation ensued.

In her teenage voice, she said, "I feel so free and filled with love. Are we here because we believed?"

Call her TJ. She wore tight jeans, a T-shirt top enhances her torso, and cowgirl boots embracing her ankles. Her eyes were alive and bright blue. When she walked, her auburn hair would sway with each step. "We have been called to freedom, to serve one another through love. We now see the light of his glory and know the mystery of truth found in the love of fellowman and wanting to treat others as we are treated. We believed and believe."

"Is this what you expected?" her companion spoke, walking alongside in short-shorts.

Call her SS. She had on a halter top, wore sandals with lengthy straps crisscrossed up her long legs. Her blackness was aglow. Her expressive face reflected her inquisitive nature.

"This is more than I expected. Truthfully I never thought I'd get past the entry point. If I made it that far, I never thought I would measure up to being able to answer the question as to my worthiness," TJ said.

It was a clear comfortable day. Not a cloud in the sky. Light filled every corner. There were no shadows. There were many walking about, smiling and greeting one another. A head would nod 'hi', or eye contact made would cause another's face to brighten. Bicyclists peddled their way about town engulfed and embraced by the healthy pollution-free air. Strollers were being gently pushed with small children's heads bobbing. Perambulators controlled by a parent's hand coasted as newborns peered up at the happy faces of their life-givers. Sidewalk cafes were occupied with coffee and tea consumers individually reading or jointly discussing events of the day or news of the times. The populace was a blend of cultures, races, and styles of dress and grooming. The stories were positive and encouraging. There was no talk of war, or terrorism, or murder, or wife beating, or civil strife. There was never a concern that at any moment a bomb might blow, a bullet might pierce the air, or a plane would explode upon impact into a nearby building. It was good news.

Fields were ablaze in the color of a vast variety of waist-high flowers in full bloom. If not flowers, uniform lawns spread across wide expanses. Play areas were set aside and maintained where joggers, kite flyers, frisbee spinners, and ballplayers were engaged in all manners of sports. Where there were winners or losers, there remained friendship and a desire to play again. Success, victory was cherished, but loss, failure, was accepted as a learning process. Exchanges were fair and the rules just. The champions embraced those that followed with respect and care for the efforts of all involved. There were children's areas where mothers or fathers, or couples, could watch their kids play, frolic, and enjoy the outdoors, the fresh air and their peers. Couples walked hand-in-hand with longing looks when they happened to gaze upon each others faces. Men and women shared the same spaces and were kind toward each other, acknowledging and respecting their sexes. It was a normal day.

There were no signs of police or military personnel among the throngs.

The same was taking place in countries and cities throughout. Many languages were being spoken, but the harmony among nations was infectious. The learning and exchange of ideas were exponential. Poverty was at a minimum and where it did exist charities were ready to more than amply provide.

Productivity was high; unemployment was at a minimum. Governments were organized and focused on the safety and security of all people, allowing for the citizens to care for each other. Government welfare was no longer necessary; their budgets were balanced and taxes in decline. Armies and security forces were at a minimum. There was transparency and honesty. There were no wars, no incursions, or surreptitious missions that needed secret funding. Talk of nuclear, chemical, or biological weapons was absent.

Looking into the windows of homes at dinnertime would find families enjoying evening meals together. The elderly were cared for by family members and/or in facilities catering to their needs deserving of the life they led and the love they had for others. Despite age, bodies are in great condition, activities continue and talk of aging issues is lacking. Obituaries were never written, as little was known of death. Was there death? People would appear and disappear without fanfare, arrivals, and departures in the normal course of events.

Love was in the air. Respect for one another was a theme. Mutual support and a desire to reach across the aisle to help another if and as needed was a common practice. All residents were color-blind in spirit, caring in nature, family oriented, and loving of neighbor. They did unto others as they would have done unto themselves in all cases, and often even more. They loved their Spiritual Guide, the Most High, with all their hearts, with all their souls, with all their minds, and with all their strength. They loved their neighbors as they loved themselves. Doors to homes were unlocked, yet residents felt secure. Trash was to each person something to be picked up, removed, and placed where it belongs. Clean streets were for everyone, enjoyed by everyone, and maintained by everyone. Illness was nonexistent. Laughing and hugging was an every day occurrence. There were no gangs and no hatred. Occasional disputes were readily resolved.

Mistakes were made, but none were made to feel guilty because of the errors. Even those who erred knew they were loved and could find comfort in the advice and solace of others. They took heed, and corrective measures taken led to improved conditions for everyone. Repentance was understood and immediate. Forgiveness was ready and adjustments were made; all lives went on without interruption.

Was this too utopian? Was there boredom that needed a boost, an escape, a conflict, or an action to create controversy?

There were no boundaries, no passports, security gates, guardhouses, or inspection stations. Drugs were unnecessary. Endorphins were secreted each day itself. Life, happiness, and smiling faces were the stimulant.

Music was important and filled the air often. Choirs, symphonies, quartets, trios, and soloists sang or produced melodies of such beauty that all desired they be heard over and over. Everyone had a voice and an ear for music and could break into song, even dance, at any moment. Instruments sang out the glory of the life they enjoyed. There was harmony.

There was one person the whole cosmos looked up to and honored. *Ram* was their king, their benefactor, their advocate, their inspiration, and the reason they were living in this eternal paradise. There were other leaders, but they too took their lead from Ram, respectful and oriented toward the common good of each and every inhabitant. The work, the effort, the toil, the accomplishments, and the successes of the residents were credited to Ram. They were productive and creative people, seeking constantly for ways to improve conditions for everyone. Much had been revealed and more would be revealed as time progressed, and as needed. To him they gave all the credit. How wonderful life was because of Ram. It could be said and shared. He walked among them without need for protection. He was a friend, a father, a teacher, a companion, a brother, and a guide.

People could gather and openly discuss their attitudes and feelings. There was no concern they would be mocked or criticized for their love of Ram, as all felt the same way and were as thankful for his loving ways. It was mutual.

It was not a society of equals, as there were those more accomplished than others, yet all gave of themselves and their abilities to enable others to be comfortable. It was from the heart and not the governing body that the population as a whole shared in the purpose for which they were designed. Life here had a purpose; it was not meaningless.

Tight-jeans TJ spoke, "We are here for a reason, I know. Are we justified for what we have received? What was it like before? Does anyone remember? There must be a story. Is this the happy ending? Is there more?"

Short-shorts SS answered, "I share in your questions. It is indeed a pleasant place. Was it always this way? We need to find one, who is able to tell us more, and provide answers. I believe I may know someone who can tell us."

"And that is?...Is it Roy, the Supreme Being, the Spiritual Guide?"

"Well, I would certainly think he would know...for sure, but no, another," SS replied.

"And that would be...?" TJ stopped and turned to face SS.

"Well...it's Mike. Let's ask Mike."

"SS, you lead the way. I will follow."

They headed to the cathedral and the room of letters. The cathedral stood out among all the buildings by its multitude of spires. They reached high as inverted icicles glowing in the light in blues and grays, whites and pinks—a prism of reflected light radiating in every direction. The structure housed a sanctuary where the Supreme Being often spoke and the populace gathered frequently, especially on the first day of the week. Entry was through a mighty arched door that remained open, accessed by way of an expanse of steps. Inside, there were offices and public spaces, to include a library within which was found the room of letters. This is where Mike was to be located.

SS and TJ climbed the stairs. They entered and found their way to the library. Through the walnut framed opening they spotted Mike hunched over his work. Piles of papers were on each side of him. SS pointed and said, "That's Mike."

Mike's head popped up from his desk, peering over one pile, he spoke, "Can I help you?"

Mike was an Ontologic that had been through the entire dimension of life as formed, as lived, as destined, and as it is now. SS, her lilting cheerful voice filling the air, "Mike, you know Ram well. You serve Roy. TJ and I would find it kind if you could relate to us our history."

When approached Mike was somewhat resistant.

"This is TJ." SS introduced her, as TJ's eyes met Mike's. "I'm SS."

Mike thought, *what should I say, but then again this needs to be shared.*

"You need to come with me."

He rose, the girls followed as they walked toward another area at the rear of the library, to another room.

There was an individual in the realm that was Ram's historian—the record keeper. He was an inspiration to those who arrived in this place. This record keeper's name was Paul. Paul worked in a room filled with books bound in wood and leather, spiral bound, with hard and soft covers, as well as paperbacked. There were scrolls and piles of loose papers. He sat at a large desk with a computer, pens, and tablets at the ready. He wore round dark tortoise shell-colored glasses. He wore what seemed to be a uniform of gray. His age was in the early 30s, but that was a guess. He was alert and welcoming. He stood as the three entered.

Mike asked, "Can you share the events of our history with these chosen two?"

SS and TJ turned toward each other with a similar quizzical expression, *chosen?*

When asked by Mike to tell the events of history Paul would readily agree. But only Mike could share the earliest events that preceded the dawn of humans.

The two began to share.

From Nothing We Begin

Mike began; Paul provided commentary as they shared.

ooooo

This is the story of our existence. It is not without turmoil or controversy, but it contains much love. The ending is a happy one. I have already given it away. Many sagas and scripts follow a similar pattern, not all having a happy outcome. It is complex and involved, but the main character is the human, the one for whom Terra exists. Follow the twists and turns, the characters, their roles, and discover the wonder of Terra.

In the beginning, in an incomprehensible void where there was neither darkness nor light, expecting no one, expecting nothing, an eternity without beginning and without end, an event took place. A call rang out, neither clarion nor bell. It was as sonar pinging off the hull of those to be assembled. A fellowship of souls gathered. They only knew they were—their direction and pathway was guided. We know not if they had eyes to see; for what was there to see? They sensed each others presence.

One of the earliest arrivals asked, "You are here too. This is quite the collection. What do you think is happening?"

"Don't know. But when the Great Soul calls we respond," a faithful follower, seeming as a small but distinct cloud, answered.

"There are more expected. This is going to be eventful," said another uniquely shaped cloud.

Only voices were heard, as nothing was seen. Clouds in a void are but drops of water in an ocean.

"Yes, I can sense the arrivals."

Another voice, another obscure mass, "Why is the council being formed?"

"I'm sure there are good reasons. He always has good reasons and good ideas."

A collection of indistinguishable beings, the Ontologics, were assembled in what can only be described as…well, simply it cannot be described except in human terms, and then only as speculation and imagination. It was as a computer cloud; it is there but where, it is unseen yet knowable. It is an invisible container, unreachable and untouchable.

They awaited the Great Soul.

More arrived and there was more chatter. No real meaning in what was said, just greetings and questions as to what was to transpire. In our terms it would be as rumblings of thunder from above, evident but muffled, a distant drum beat, beat, beat, in the course of a developing or far off storm. All that was discernable from the podium, a sense of a large assemblage, were the Ontologics, the *beings* of an eternal vacuum.

Suddenly, without the fanfare that would be expected upon the entry of a president, before the throng, appeared, an essence sensed. It was the Great Soul, an all encompassing, magnetic, charismatic, and commanding presence. He was an electrical current pulsing, but unseen. A static electrical charge had built up as the Ontologics compressed which released when the Great Soul took his position. He was seated as was his custom, yet how would they know. The released static spark turned them all in the correct direction. Facing in all directions the crowd quieted down and turned toward, as a compass pointing north, the Great Soul.

It was for you and me as looking into an amorphous mass—a picture painted of a reality not human, but to be visualized to understand. The scene: a cloud gathering in a sea of grey, dark, hazy, and without definition; the components of little meaning. However, what was about to occur was meaningful to all of mankind.

The Great Soul whom the crowd referred to reverently as Roy, spoke. The voice was eloquent, deep, resonant, and clear, "*We* know you have questions," he paused to insure all were attentive, "as *we* do not have this type of meeting often."

He looked around and said, "*We* have been contemplating our reality and have a presentation *we* need you all to hear. There are going to be changes. You may have wondered about your presence. This will now define us all and provide a role, as players on a large stage."

Sensations, senses, as eyes were darting one to another and back toward Roy, most alert to the speaker, intently focused on the next words to be spoken. They knew the *we*.

"Behold," the Great Soul announced, pausing to insure all were keenly alert, "*We* will need the help of every one of you... listen." There was silence.

The sensory eyes were wide with the raising of a perceived eyebrow over a socket, a grey shadow oval indent in the marshmallow form. For a human, the depression would contain an eye. It was clear the next words would be heard.

"*We* are now ready to make something unique. All our skills are to be put into action. *We* need you to be ready. Your training will prove most valuable. Each of you will have specific functions. There will be a structure and order to what is about to occur. *We* have mapped out a plan. As you may have noticed our numbers are static. *We* need more like you. With more it will be better. You are all good, and, at times, we have our differences, but you are in harmony and we can grow in numbers. *We* will be forming an incubator that will produce such as you."

An arm rose from the audience, more an escape of a gaseous nature as a plume. It was a broadcasting antenna, communicating, from a member of the audience, sensed and acknowledged by Roy.

The Ontologic asked, "Why? We have not had such a need before."

"Thank you for asking. *We* know. However, this is what *we* want, there are reasons; there is room and more can follow," responded the Great Soul.

At the same time he considered what could happen, canvassing by feel his associates, and compelled by a need to determine who among them was with him or possibly against him. This would be the test. The burden would be mostly on Roy. His use of moral discernment was as nothing else. His judgment was the most sound. He would need to maintain discipline and order, so the process to begin and continue would occur without incident.

Silence filled the locale. It was still, as if the assembly was but a single body whose heart stopped.

"The objective…" Roy began. The distinct sound of his voice called all to attention.

He continued after some time…"The facts to occur will be obvious. Those who cannot accept what we do have no excuse. Their refusal will be a topic of conversation, debate, and study. It will be their blindness…The evidence will be plain…."

Another antenna, a burst from amid the throng, transmitted, "Will you be known?

Roy answered, "Known, yes. Believed, that should be your concern. Believing in me will be accompanied with doubt, and or denial, by those who cannot or refuse to see….Let us proceed."

ooooo

From this nothingness, this void, the quiet, the emptiness we have the beginning. In the beginning….

We often wonder why and what are we doing here on Terra, hanging in space. Time passes and many have passed, literally, before us. Terra, third rock from the sun, is our paradise, our home, our life-support module, and more than a meaning to everyone. Terra is the ship carrying us in space, well equipped and seemingly perpetual, its power source assured, and the food supplies sufficient. Life continues, replenishing itself with new life, and training new captains and crew. Where we are headed, our purpose, however, often comes into question.

We can appreciate our surroundings, the pets, other animals, the trees and flowers, and certainly food—home cooking, fast food and fine dining. We explore and are enamored by what we see that has no end, peering into infinite space when we look up. Bright during the day, star-studded at night on the good days, but exciting and scary with lightning and thunder, rain, hail, and clouds, and reports of tornados, hurricanes, typhoons, and tsunamis touching down on not so good days. It remains a wonder.

We wake, we sleep; we need rest. Newborns, society, politics, government, friends, and family, persons with whom we have relationships all provide information. What does it say? What are we being told? Is there an explanation? Who built this ship we are on? From whence came the sea of space, nebula, stars, planets, suns, moons, and galaxies in which we travel?

You are about to embark on a journey—a journey with Roy, an eternal force in a place beyond knowing. He is unchanging. You will be enlightened by his story. May you discover more about your place, the place you live, and your place in where you live.

You may and should believe Roy, knowing what you will now learn.

ooooo

Roy is the leading personality, the Great Soul, an Ontologic of enormous character with great credentials and a superb work ethic. His character is one of responsible oversight for his fellow associates. Roy is unique to the Ontologic—as a composite, an essence as one with a persona with different functions. He is the *we*. Labeling the personas as "functionaries", each functionary is fully Roy having all the attributes of Roy, equal as the being—an Ontologic. The purpose of each functionary of a composite of *one* has one as the planner, one as the implementer, and one that manifests and sustains what was planned and implemented.

Unexplainable, yet to the Ontologic there is no contradiction. Roy will always be a mystery to the humans. Roy refers to himself as *we* and *our* to reflect the functionaries, as much as he uses the pronoun, *I.* Together they comprise the unity of the head of the dimension in which all Ontologics now dwell.

Roy has patience. As the chief engineer in the fifth dimension, a separate dimension apart from anything, we know or can conceive. Existing before space and time, incomprehensible actions were taken as scientist, anthropologist, manipulator, and every other form of medical, mental, or research professional—Roy is all one can be.

Roy dwells in a locale completely independent from matter and energy, the laws and constants of physics, and the space-time dimension of the cosmos. His freedom to operate and invent knows no boundaries.

Roy operates from a throne on wheels, always seated, always ready, and always working. He has a myriad of controllers at hand, capable of delivering him instantly anywhere. As if in a mobile omni-control center, an elaborate vehicle powered by multiple supernatural computers, Roy manages with absolute authority. He is the *cloud* that can be called upon by the human mind at anytime, anywhere, asked or not.

Roy is not a being as our mind might see; his form is not intelligible. His ways are unlike our ways. In his dimension, there are others under his command, some almost equals, but Roy is in charge and has been. There were those whose council Roy respected, they too had thrones, and all were dressed in white obscuring formations with crowns of imagined gold. From their command post, with columns of large lamps lining their room, the light bright and the hum of activity heard, they peered into the distance as through a glass wall. These council members would not be recognizable to humans, as they were like friendly creatures but as *beings* in a form man has never even contemplated.

In this realm there is no change; it is eternal. It is the Dimension Eternal (DE). Roy embodies all philosophy, psychology, and science. He is the *master*—as well as planner, agent and representative. Roy had an idea, a vision, a liberating concept, and shared it with his associates. The only way Roy could describe his objective was to point to himself.

ooooo

"*The objective*," Roy's vibrato began, "is to engender a cosmos containing a foundational basis upon which a living body, many bodies, with traits that are special can dwell. They will be *our* workmanship, able to think, remember, reproduce, care for each other, love and hate, and understand what is theirs to oversee.

"I can only conceive something in my likeness. Also I have good works for them to do, and I will prepare them in advance. We too will live among them, have the pleasure of their company and a relationship with them. Markers will be provided that as discovered will continuously reveal the truth. There is a plan. I am the necessary element in making the plan happen."

"Well", the associates responded, many mumbling in a harmonious tremolo, "that will take some doing. Much will be needed. As the source of all, how will you start?"

"Thank you." was the *master's* reply. With confidence he spoke, "Step one, we will need two essentials—*time* and *space*.

"Time? What is *time*?" queried one of the council members, his feather plume extended.

"This you need to understand. With such a beginning a measure of existence will be enabled. Using time we will have a starting point and that will allow for an end. An alpha and an omega. It will not be infinite. As the process unfolds any point in time, a *yom*, a day, will only occur with a start. Time will only be able to go back to its first tick; it will not be able to go back indefinitely. Each second or moment used will be gone forever.

"So *time*—it will be the basis of measurement providing the point at which we start for that which we cause. Time will allow a reference point for all to follow, from which all will follow. We never alter. We know only now an eternity without a scale for which there is no beginning and there is no end. There needs to be in that which we cause a past and then only can there be a future. This is to be called time. As to the start and the end of time, I am that. My word I give and time will be," Roy answered.

Another plume spewed forth, "Okay, then—What about *space*?"

"Space, well, we…we are without dimension, infinite, eternal, and always existing. We are un-seeable yet we are that which is required to make that which is wonderful. The entity will need definition, a location, a place of its own, not eternal as ours, but with boundaries, with an ability to sustain itself for as long as *we* decide. That will be called *space*. It too, as time, can be caused and it will exist and *we* will provide that which is necessary for it to continue. All that is necessary I will provide. My word I give and space will be."

"Is there more?" Many antennas beamed as smoke.

"Yes, of course—there will be *life*.

"Life?"

"*Life* is what will be the objective—time and space to be used to cause the conditions to support life—beings. Beings, Ontologics, not as us, but having elements from us." Roy peered over his gathered council. He sensed concern.

"Listen to me." The organ that was the source of Roy's vocal output was expressive.

"I know this may be a bit confusing; it is all so new, but bear with me. There is a purpose to my plan, which includes the cosmos to be developed and the ultimate life-form. What you may sense as complex, the life *we* make possible, the beings, will find even more complex. We will know life, but life which *we* will make in *our* image. I conceive and we will need to discover and embrace the reality that was needed to make life possible. As the overseer, the I am, with your aid, we will be helpful in all ways to the life *we* give."

They were listening, compressed as a tightly filled jar of cotton, totally engaged in what Roy was saying.

Roy continued, "It will be a process, and you must know there will be justification for each stage. Our work will not be easy; that you must accept. It may take more to embody this life than there will be time, as that life knows to continue to exist. There may even be multiple stages, each with a function; in fact, as I envision it there will be six major steps.

"We will have to make ready the environment for the living bodies, capable of life support, to include food stuffs and other creatures. Then, when all is ready, the living body will be put into place. Readiness is essential. Once all is done and enabled for the living Ontologic we conceive, the anthropic parameters fully established, species and kinds will become animated, and my breath will fill their forms.

"The forces necessary to sustain life and engender reproduction will be in place. The ultimately *caused* body will then have responsibility for everything that comes prior so that it can go on. There will be a most responsible being placed in charge of all the others. They will have the job of continuing what is made for them. If I really like what I design, the living elements, possibly at the end some can become part of our team.

"And you know that without us there would be no cause for what is to occur. I will be, and, thus, am, the cause. I am needed so this can take place. It is a daunting task, but offers the opportunities for many lifetimes to be fulfilled and for us to determine additional associates to join us in this eternal place. My word I give and life will be."

As the brightest of signals from a large lighthouse Roy's words were directive, "Let's get started."

The associates replied, "It's all up to you, Roy. You are the source upon which all will be dependent."

"I tell you this—our objective, when this is all finished and I relax, is to have a place where I will dwell and live among those living creatures to which I will equip with a functioning bodily system and enable them to maintain this new place for themselves, as well as sustain and improve upon it for other similar living creatures that follow. You all must help me with this and play your part.

"It will be much different than what you now know. You too will have specific roles to play and will be used on many occasions to visit and provide clarion calls for those living to hear, obey, and understand. Those, with whom I reside and all of the surroundings, including other occupants and life-support elements will have a job, a function, and a use.

"There will be a purpose for everything. Without a purpose there would be no rational explanation for what we're about to do or for those placed in this new environment. It would be meaningless, meaningless, meaningless. We will only do what is possible for me. Critical will be a living being capable of emulating me in many ways, all in fact except one, and to have a relationship with me, so together, even though I will be the ultimate voice, the controller, we can continue to improve on the new place. What is possible for me may not be possible for the living beings *we* cause. Also, *our* presence will be among those which we establish."

"There will be freedom," Roy continues.

"We will call this new place *Terra*."

"The space that surrounds Terra, call it the *cosmos*, will also have a purpose to provide for the living creatures—all life forms. That which is provided is the breath I give."

The associates-in-mass carefully interrupted Roy's sermon, "How will you live among them? How will they know?"

"Good Question," Roy answered.

He then thought for a second and said, "They will know first that I know them. They will know too the *wonders* they see and experience as needed, for their existence are not of their doing. My presence will be elusive, yet the reality of *our* achievements we will make known to them. *We* will leave *markers* also; the markers will enable those living which *we* equip with the ability to conceptualize to see *our* handiwork, and even make improvements as *we* deem necessary.

"They will know there must be an eternal nature to engender, to begin the time-constrained wonder. They will know that which *is* and must be, no name, although a nature that is needed, that is the source of all being, that is the source of all that is true and relevant. Their future will be uncharted, but they will know they need to follow guidelines *we* will provide, to follow that which *is*. I am *is*."

Roy lovingly embraced his gathered council taking in the strength-field of each representative.

"Not all will understand. They will never explain this beginning; they will avoid the answer that is obvious. There should be no doubt, but frankly I know better. But my plan will stand firm forever. You'll see. *We* will deal with the ungrateful nonbeliever."

"One last item," Roy said ending his proclamation, "your position in our realm is vital, unique, and glorious. You will be useful as informer, communicator, and interpreter. You will do your part in providing oversight, feedback, and defending the plan. This will all seem like a grand party with a need for many hosts and hostesses. You will be the hosts of Roy. As the need arises you will be asked to serve in other ways as well. Be prepared."

With outstretched embracing elements from the image Roy clearly projected, his words boomed, "And now we begin."

Wonders

Roy applied his talents, with the aid of his Ontologic associates, and 13.73 billion years ago (as measured by humans) time and space, as we know it, were initiated and like a balloon began to expand. Think also of a tent arising out of nowhere, filling space.

A continuous blast of material as from a vacuum on reverse was heading in every direction. The blast was more an *event* than an explosion. The distribution of matter and energy was part of the starting point of this engineered product. From a primordial point, a concentrated product of the highest possible density, in an instant, the turn of a dial on the mobile omni-control center, a verbal command, a snap of Roy's finger, a boom of ear-shattering proportions, if anyone was there to hear, and cosmos initiation occurred. Then there was *space*. This was *wonder*.

The Ontologics were observing and gasped in unison at Roy's igniting of the cosmos. *Ooohh's* and *aaahhs* were mumbled. Energy, heretofore, an unknown was now known.

The resulting energy from what Roy caused was optimized. The expanding ball of cosmological stuff had to be controlled. The Ontologics were used to surround the blast radius and monitor under Roy's instructions. Insufficient energy and the cosmos would collapse on itself. The construction of the elements required for life would need time. Too much energy and the density and gravitational pull of the material elements formed would have prevented necessary star formations. There would be a place and time for everything. A glorious ball of energy and matter illuminates this new space as a display of endless fireworks finales. Yom one came to a close.

ooooo

As this eruption occurred Roy's associates for the first time experienced contrasts. They discovered an ability to see as well as sense. It was the result of dark and light now exposed from a void of unknown composition, if anything at all.

"What is going on?" they asked as would a deaf or blind man with the instant realization they could hear or see. It was glorious.

Roy responded, "Do not be afraid. We need what we will refer to as light. This will be as much a marvel to the engineering that will occur as all else. It is an awakening, an opening of eyes you never knew you had, the ability to see—a new reality. The opposite is darkness. There will be a contrast from light or white to grey to black or dark. There will be color. In color there is beauty and the excitement of seeing so much more than what you sense.

"What you may sense, our revealed cosmos, will be confirmed through organs that can visualize, can see, and can distinguish the actual. Light will remove shadows or that which cannot be seen, cannot be fully comprehended. Light and dark will fill the void. Light is revelation. In the presence of light all will be known, unless you are otherwise blind. In the light you will see truth. In the darkness there is only speculation, confusion, a lack of direction, and doubt."

Satisfied, the associates continued their work with a new excitement, with eyes to see, inspired, and anxious to be part of Roy's ongoing process.

ooooo

Separate protons, neutrons, and electrons, the fundamental particles, were present in a mix called ylem. The temperature was extreme, the electrons moving too fast to combine, to attach, and form a nucleus. Everything was present as if in a fog, an opaque light, chaotic and luminescent.

In a very short period of time, five minutes or three hundred thousand years, during which there was nothing but gas, energy, radiation, and waves of electromagnetic forces, as if so little time and so much energy, enough cooling took place for nucleosynthesis to begin. Atoms were forming. The atoms were foundational. From lesser particles, sub-particles – quarks, mesons, pions or kaons, and leptons—atoms were structured. Each could be numbered.

Helium and hydrogen appeared within seconds and filled space. Atoms of deuterium and tritium were also produced. The periodic table of the elements was evolving. They were eventually numbered.

In the earliest billion or so years many exploding events took place. There were super-novas bursting from multiple stars. Even a sun—a star larger than our *sun* erupted—announcing its destruction and death. From the stuff of supernovas came elements such as gold and uranium. Energy abounded as this cosmic event took place. Sky became more abundant. A cycle of light and dark, or less light, remained as periods of new time passed. Moisture was present in the amalgam of space particles.

Evidence of this remnant light from a period soon after the start-up process would be left as a fossil record of the initiation of the cosmos. Roy knew someday the record of this occurrence would become known.

Only Roy and his cohorts could view this glorious exhibition. But it did brighten the area newly formed.

"How are we doing so far?" Roy asked.

In exclamation his cohorts, their mouths agape, tears of excitement in their eyes said, "It is all so spectacular, and well done!"

Roy and his friends watched, observed, and exchanged thoughts as this conflagration of particles filled this newness of space within a new timeframe. Billions of years went by—as if in a photo flash. Pieces of space stuff joined together separated and grew. Accretion material formed inanimate bodies.

The *engineer* was at work to establish a place where life could be formed and could exist. He knew from what was growing that there would be one particle that he could further develop to support an embodiment of himself. He did what was necessary at each step of the way. Time for Roy, in a class of his own, without limits, eternal, was of little consequence, it was possibly days, years, eons, or Yoms, and for many of us it was incomprehensible time periods interpreted as only days.

He carefully observed all that was transpiring. What would be a mystery to many would also be revealing to many. Clues were left behind.

After 9.1 billion years, this cosmos of particles had grown and one essential piece to his puzzle found. Established among the many bodies that emerged from the starting blocks of the cosmos was a molten space rock. Roy gathered his associates, his helpers, and made note of the vessel that would contain their primary focus. Objective realities were forming. Gravity was pulling and pushing. A rapid expansion was slowing.

He proclaimed, as only Roy could, "this molten form will be ordered in a fashion to house life. Our energies will be directed toward this hot rock."

Each associate was assigned tasks, given responsibility to observe and manipulate specific elements enabling the wonder they were informed would occur to take shape. They lined up, a long procession, of what looked like white Smurfs, to take their orders in total obedience to Roy. Their mushroom remained Roy's kingdom.

This molten form they watched boiling, flaming, and flailing in space was to be Terra.

Another Wonder. It was a focal point of Roy's good efforts.

More space hot rocks would combine, collide, and combine to grow Terra. The make-up of Terra are atoms, atoms formed into the shape Roy desired. He could do much with atoms.

Underneath the atom was a particle of Roy's making mass possible. All will come together according to plan.

Dark baryonic matter, non-baryonic stuff, neutrinos, axions, and other terrestrial objects occupied the ever expanding cosmos arena. Stellar cauldrons boiling over produced essential elements. Some particles moved slowly, others at the speed of light. Stellar cores cooled. Cold dark matter streamed virtually unobstructed from stars bringing energy into the equation. Matter occupied 30 percent and dark energy 70 percent of the growing area of space.

Galaxies formed like an army of gladiators fighting for their own dominion—many, many galaxies. One of the many was chosen in which to further develop Terra. It was a spiral galaxy, snail shaped, distributed in the cosmos as a band of light formed in a dark theater, a celestial sphere comprised of endless light sources, cosmic pieces. Those pieces we refer to as stars. The Murky Way formed, swirling yet flat in appearance as if a hand coated with wet paint brushed a wall creating a noticeable and fixed array. It is the galaxy in which our solar system and Terra dwells. Over 200 billion stars formed the Murky Way. And beyond the Murky Way would be even more galaxies. In time, over a hundred billion galaxies.

For the record, and to further our understanding, Terra has been labeled, by man, by its dating from the present. Terra 4.63B means Terra 4.63 billion years ago. B is for billion, followed by M for million and T for thousand.

ooooo

When it was complete, Roy saw major events as *good*.

When we attempt to gaze into the wonder of the inception of the cosmos, it can only be followed by the *wonder* of the inception of Terra. Only Roy could do what has been done.

All of this work, what came before and was to come, would be the result of a designing mind and a designing hand. The cosmos became the potter's wheel upon which Terra's physical evolution would continue.

Not perfect, this structure for Terra needed further serious attention before life as we know it could occur. It was a ball of molten, boiling rock, an amalgam of rapidly moving atoms bouncing off each other and following instructions. In time, like a pie, much of the center core gelled containing essential fruits of the planet. A crust formed a solid covering over both a molten and hard body. Heavy elements were in the center and lighter elements were on top. More were needed—essential chemicals and minerals. A specific position in the space arena, within the Murky Way, had to be located.

Roy's objective included a relative stability of location, essential deposits of materials to one day enable growth, appropriate atmospheric conditions, a balance of greenhouse gases to protect the temperature tolerances required and oxygen. All were critical support items for living organisms.

Absorbing and emitting radiation, the greenhouse effect, needed to be controlled. Too little and Terra could be too cold; too much Terra could be too hot. Terra 4.63B was the beginning of a mass that would eventually support life. Random up to that point the choice of Terra 4.63B was intentional.

This piece of matter in the time-space dimensional cosmos by Roy, Terra, had a purpose. Further transformation was required. To work perfectly all elements to sustain life needed development, coordination, and adjustments.

ooooo

The space enveloping Terra filled with moisture. The internals of Terra filled with moisture. Light appeared. Then darkness. Light anew. Darkness to follow. The cycle continued. Moisture increased—above and within Terra. Yom two was ending.

ooooo

In the expanding space of the Murky Way, space particles moved indiscreetly passing at high speeds. On many occasions they were imperceptibly close to other space particles. Particles merged, collided, and grew in size. They became more ominous also in their potential to crash into space stuff. Terra was at risk.

Suddenly....

A space object collided with Terra.

The *associates* watched with great anticipation. Had they lost control? Did they err? Turning toward Roy one asked, "What is happening now?"

It was soon after its formation, only 3–4 billion years passed (a short period in eternal time) when a sizable object, the size of today's Mars, struck at a 45° angle.

It was as if Roy seeing all these objects floating on a three dimensional billiard table had a pool cue in hand. He took careful aim, calculating, adjusting, and when ready perfectly executed his shot moving one choicely selected ball-like object, molten at that, at the correct angle and trajectory toward Terra to carom precisely and deflect into position, as falling into a side pocket. It was a space-pocket.

Terra moved, its surface moved, and its orbit was altered.

"There! Now we have Terra where we need it." Roy sighed.

He turned toward the Ontologics. "What we have done is *good.*"

Making Adjustments—the Bombardment

Like many different colorful horses, elephants, benches, and swans on a carousel, circling the center pole, a large quantity of comets, meteors and asteroids were circling Terra. In this case, however, it was a dense ring around the rosy fireball of the molten rock of Terra. Collisions of terrestrial matter caused flaming detritus from dead stars.

During the next billion years Terra was bombarded. Boom, bang, crash, thud, and all you can conjure up in words to describe sudden hits and explosions resulted from impact after impact. If there were ears to hear the sounds would be deafening and continuous. While remaining in its position the constant collisions caused a buildup of matter from falling, and cascading comets, meteors, and asteroids.

The circling variegated bodies when captured by the gravitational attraction of Terra disintegrated while descending. The remnants deposited caused this planet to grow. Many were simply large ice formations depositing oceans and lakes. Instantly, water-laden clouds were generated from the vaporizing steam upon contact with molten rock. Mile high tsunamis moved land and made hills. Chemicals, minerals, new to Terra, were deposited. The atmosphere changed along with Terra's thickness. Essential iron levels grew, magnetic fields were formed and cosmic rays and solar-X rays where shielded. Water vapor became more and more abundant.

From the whirlwind of the furnace of space, a sizable object, as large as one thousand or more junkyards full of discarded school buses, greater than what heretofore bombed Terra, struck. Kaboom! The rotation of the planet was altered. Oddly enough it became somewhat more stable. Light became more optimum, increasingly correct for the needs of life, and more predictable. Radiation was intense. Temperatures were being adjusted, the unimaginable million degree extremes mitigated, as manageable temperature ranges became an objective need.

Roy's Associates were doing their job. Roy was pleased.

It all took fine-tuning and time, but the result was good. So far so good, but more were necessary. Terra was dry in areas, wet in areas, and a form of vegetation appeared under conditions quite severe, unimaginable. There was no rain, but there was moisture. It was the end of Yom three.

ᴜᴜᴜᴜᴜ

The colliding space object that struck and positioned Terra bounced off, gathering excess debris with it, moved away, and established an orbit around Terra. It became Terra's *moon*. The *moon* settled into a synchronized pattern of continuous movement with Terra. This *moon* collision slowed the rotation of Terra. The gravitation effect of the moon and Terra on each other was symbiotic. The *moon* was critical too in its appearance, effect, and protection of Terra. Although residing in a sterile vacuum the *moon* had an anthropological purpose along with Terra.

Terra's movement in space, hanging as an object on a decorated tree, but without hooks, rotating, was wobbly at best. It began to settle into a pattern, a repeatable turning action.

An object producing heat and light became a regular occurrence in the rotating cycle. In the myriad of bright and shining objects in the Murky Way, one in particular became a center for the orbit in which Terra traveled. Other cosmic stuff also orbited this bright centerpiece. The *moon's* orbit stayed with Terra. This point of intense fiery matter illuminated and warmed the side of Terra facing the object. As Terra turned on its own axis, the rays and warmth traveled over its surface. This bright star in the cosmos became Terra's sun. A star, Terra's star, was to provide in conjunction with other items in space day and night and the correct temperatures right for life.

All was progressing according to Roy's plan: life, the goal.

Terra required an efficient orbit around the *sun*. At the same time, the necessary and most important *sun* had many of the bodies in space drawn to it, a gravitational attraction, as a central core.

Terra now had a moon that influenced its place in the cosmos and a sun, along with the dark, to heat and cool the surface. Together they would operate to cause the optimum conditions for Roy's plan. Modifications allowed for Terra and the *moon* to orbit the *sun* in concert with each other. The mathematics of the relationship of these objects in space became calculable. Relativity became determinable and solar physics was born.

Yom four was *good*.

ooooo

Roy was smart and left a footprint which today enables astronomers using instruments like the Bubble telescope to peer into distant space without interference or obstacles in the way. In view would be the start of his engineering feat, the magnificence of Roy's work-in-progress. The astronomers would conclude too that all that exist are finite, having a beginning, and there will be an end—but when? Galaxies beyond our own are also visible. The space between each is expanding, a proof of the nature of Terra's cosmos. The galaxies were present in the primordial point from which Roy began this process. The best possible viewing position for his effort was Terra.

Red-shift analysis, a study and calculation of the stretching, the elongation of space, enabled measurements of distant galaxies to Terra. The longest wavelength of electromagnetic radiation, that of the gamma ray, is detectible in the red end of the light spectrum ranging from dark blue or black to red. The frequency of the gamma ray is the shortest. Its wiggle factor is less than the other electromagnetic waves (when measured against time) ranging from radio waves (highest wiggle factor or frequency and shortest wavelength—the gamma ray having the lowest frequency and the longest wavelength). Visible light is also a form of electromagnetic radiation near the middle of the range. It can be seen, whereas the others, to include microwave and UV (ultraviolet) radiation are not visible.

Roy would enable intellects, astro-scientists, mathematicians and physicists to calculate his work and gain knowledge for specific life-forms to use in further understanding the planet Terra. He was aware too there were those that would look at the *wonder* of it all in amazement and be thankful for the *engineering*. Duplicating this work, though, was the purview of only Roy. He is alone in having the know-how, the awareness, to make Terra and to form the atoms in ways suitable for his purposes.

Roy's revelation could be understood and would be understood as necessary.

ooooo

The bombardment continued, but at a declining rate. Hundreds of thousands of pounds of extraterrestrial debris was vaporized and deposited with a thunderous impact, with further accumulations from post vaporization fallout on every square yard of Terra's surface.

About Terra 3.875B there was a great bombardment burst of such magnitude the intensity would have destroyed anything in its path. Thousands of hits, often daily, were taking place. It was a fundamental salting of Terra with heavy elements. The belt of comets, meteors, and asteroids became less populated and the threat to Terra eventually diminished greatly. The bombardment burst lasted from start to end almost 1.5 billion years. At the end it was Terra 3.8B. At the end of the bombardment tirade all became quiet.

Still there was no life on Terra. Terra's orbit was stabilized. The *sun* appeared in a predictable and measured fashion. The *moon* showed its face at night—at times, full but most often in part, a shadow of Terra hiding its total surface. Terra positioned between the *sun* and the *moon*. It was a time as if after a terrible storm that continued for days ended, out of the covers of your bed you emerged to be greeted with a dawn, the sky clear, the sun rising and bright. You looked up, cautious at first, but then more confident that it would be a nice day. Thankful, too, that the storm was over.

"Are we any closer to your goal?" Roy was asked.

"Just wait. Have patience. You'll see."

Suddenly things changed in a shudder, as an unexpected, uncontrollable shaking from a chill. From the depths of sulfur-filled acidic bubbling seas to locations on the surface, Roy was laying down his coded essence in a vast variety of strange organisms. Green shoots sprung up straining and gasping.

As if in an instant there was life. On cue. In its simplest form life appeared—multiple unicellular life-forms, not one but many, possibly. Due to the oxygen-ultraviolet paradox, these life-forms were not chemical or environmental precursors of the origin of life—human basics. At this stage there was too little oxygen, too much radiation, no ozone layer. The deficiency of needed elements halted essential biological formations. No amino acids, critical to the chemistry of life-forms, was present. These were elements of life, in place, early stages of the development, staging and shaping continuum. In its simplest form the first evidence of life was complex, irreducibly so.

In less than a few million years Terra changed from a life terminator to a life generator. Roy had accomplished much.

More engineering remained before advanced life-forms would be plausible.

"We are progressing. We are building the foundational elements. It is coming together," Roy noted.

The two major collision events were part of the plan and necessary—the moon and the bombardment. Terra was made alive. More like we know it, Terra had dry land, seas and rivers, islands and lakes, and spots of vegetation, but little else.

Testing was ongoing, trial and error methods employed using intentionally designed codes to produce the most functional living machinery. The earliest models were primitive and fine-tuned to the existing environment. The most optimal designs were used anew. What worked well for one type was retained and would work well for another, redesigned or improved only for the next intended purposeful life-type. Advanced life was yet to come. Challenges remained.

To make life habitable by humans, it would take many, many millions, billions of years (3,799,950,000 years estimated by today's man). Roy was still at work making Terra ready for his master plan. Gradually the code for human life was being introduced. Food stuffs were needed. The bombardment provided a foundation for some resources, but more were required, that would take time. Roy had time.

By now Roy called for the proper coordination of the *sun* and *moon* providing greater and lesser light. The *sun's* rays, the greater, became Terra's dominant light source, illuminating, warming, and irradiating its surface. The lesser was the night filled with sparkles of stars, stars as numerous as the sand of Terra's beaches. It was a dazzling array of mini and maxi suns filling infinite space surrounding Terra. The cosmos of speckles of night-light was part of Roy's spectacular capabilities on display. It provided dimension and scenery for the emptiness in which Terra was located.

ooooo

Today the cosmos is comprised of 4 percent matter in the form of atoms, 23 percent cold dark matter and 73 percent dark matter, but what matters the most is the matter of Terra.

ooooo

Expanses of water, seas, and oceans formed, altered, ever changing, but the simplest creatures lived and died and made useful deposits. New life-forms, seed-bearing plants, vegetation, and trees appeared when they could be supported. Each had their own code, a formula useful and similar, a combination that worked but containing common elements. Roy sought efficiency. He desired as few spare parts as possible.

There have often been sudden, surprisingly sudden appearances of various species, different kinds of plant life. As changes took place existing life-forms became extinct and new ones came to be. Signs of sea life were in evidence, birds too—all different kinds. They were limited, supplied in stages, replaced as needed, in an effort to develop those fish and birds more accommodating to man and most suitable to Terra and the conditions of Terra at any given moment in time.

By introducing new kinds and eliminating old as needed, Roy adjusted the nature of the species. Using similar ingredients from Roy's pantry and tested recipes, Roy was able to introduce a variety of living matter. Getting everything just right was not easy. Roy applied the Goldilocks objective—making adjustments, often too much or too little, but just right was the goal.

Periods of mass extinction took place, taking situations to extremes. The debris left behind decayed and developed as part of today's coal and oil deposits and other future needs for man. Underground organisms useful and helpful to the process of decay were brought into action. Roy was building required resources and inventories for man.

Greenhouse gas adjustments were prompted. More carbon dioxide or less, more water vapor or less, the *sun* more luminous and less, levels raised and lowered, it was a process. Ice ages caused by too little greenhouse gases came and went, the surface of Terra altered, surface conditions changed, the soil and ground mixture became a better feeder for living organisms. Terra cooled and warmed. Changes in the greenhouse effect took place well before the advent of humans. Oxygen was also vital, in tightly managed ranges, to aid life—human life.

Sponges and jellyfish were in evidence in studies of animal fossils, the oldest found, on Terra 575M, the Avalon Explosion, 575 million years ago. Today's paleontologists were provided clues to Roy's handiwork in the fossil records left behind. It was a view, a picture, of Yom five; Yom six as well. More was to be learned.

ooooo

Thirty million years passed, Terra 543M, the Cambrian Explosion, much more advanced life-forms appeared; fossil history had more to show as more was now possible for the *engineer to introduce*. Large plants and animals of many species are present in fossil history. It was at that time Terra was more ready for the life and purpose that it was to be given. Living creatures, many animal species were now located on the planet. Livestock, snakes, and wild animals suddenly appeared. Fossil fuel deposits increased. The *engineer* continued to build inventories that have only recently been accessed.

Millions of more years passed. Research has shown greenhouse gases, especially containing high levels of carbon dioxide, was evident in Terra 500M, ten times higher than today. Terra was hot, too hot, but the hot house helped grow plants.

At Terra 350M, a few hundred thousand years ago swamp plants were plentiful and by Terra 300M, there were forests. The high carbon dioxide concentrations fed and accelerated the presence of the abundant plant life. The plant life in turn was generating needed oxygen. Levels of oxygen were increasing, carbon dioxide decreasing, and Terra was cooling. Oxygenating Terra was difficult and required much plant life and photosynthetic life.

Now Terra is alone among the planets having such a high abundance of free oxygen in its atmosphere. Microbial soils helped in this transformation. Greenhouse gases were adjusting and Terra's temperature was moderating.

Adjusting—a constant for Roy. Picture a room lined on all sides with panels of hundreds and hundreds of dials and gauges, LCD computer screens, and joysticks. Roy and his associates are sitting before the panels in swivel chairs on wheels. Over the panels and monitors is an opening, a window to the cosmos being formed and the multitudes of things afloat in space. There is motion from one side to another, objects crossing paths with each other. Roy needed to patiently make perfect the settings, commanding others to make alterations as he sensed a need for the purpose intended for the planet of life. Critical also were distances from obstacles, planets, stars, space flotsam and jetsam, each placed with an intended relationship, often permanent, to each other. Off by the smallest of percentages and the goal of Roy would not be possible.

To exist in concert, one with another chemical levels inherent in creatures and minerals were to be of the closest conceivable tolerances. Be it salt, oxygen, hydrogen, the axis of orbiting planets, the presence of needed planets or moons one to another, if not optimized, the objective for Roy would be null and void.

"Do not be afraid," Roy would say to his associates, "this will all work when I am done. You will see. Just do as I say."

"We have confidence in you," collectively the fellows of the eternal council stated encouragingly.

The process of fine-tuning was to continue.

Paradise

Everything was going well.

But then, things went too far!

Watching their controls and the formation process, several Ontologics noticed unexpected changes. They waddled right to left, checking their window to this new arena, making minor adjustments to no avail. They became anxious and knew they needed to inform Roy. The observing associates selected two to bring this potential dilemma to Roy's attention, "Have we a problem, Roy?" They asked believing he would know.

"I'll handle this," he responded with a calming influence.

With that….

It became too cold. Snow and ice formed, greenhouse gases, carbon dioxide, decreased to very low levels. As the ice formed, solar energy was reflected. Roy was actively trying to adjust the magnetic Terra field and align the poles. The Ontologics watched intently. There was a glitch. Just prior to Terra 200M snow, slush, ice covered much of Terra. The frozen tundra surface approached the equator. Ocean surfaces appeared in thick ice masses instead of land masses. Down deep warm to hot ocean bottoms allowed living structures to continue. The equator was cold, but not frozen.

A major volcanic eruption was demanded. Roy with one motion caused explosive and expansive sub-surface contents to spew forth from a variety of locations. Fiery storms of lava flowed as steam arose from the cold and wet layers. Carbon dioxide levels rapidly increased to 350 times today's levels. The whole of

Terra warmed rapidly, the poles aligned, the ice, slush and snow receded, and the equator and tropics warmed and became hot. The plants revived, carbon dioxide was their feeder, and oxygen again was in production. Sea life sprang forth. New life-forms suddenly appeared. All was made good.

It was Terra 200M. What took one million to three million years was reversed in one thousand years. The *engineer* needed to be at the top of his game. With all he had accomplished much could have changed, but mass extinction was avoided. The Ontologics began shaking each other's hands and praising Roy.

By Terra 140M mountains were formed, the moon controlled the tides, landmass increased, all parts of the greenhouse balancing act. Magically as if in fast-speed camera action a rainbow of colors, a garden of pluralistic flowers opened, bloomed, and cried out in color. Roy liked beauty. The great patience of the *engineer* was obvious. Roy even saw in nature's garden a way of revealing himself. Sea creatures came next in abundance and then animals, birds, dogs, horses, mammals were walking on Terra. The animate life varieties appeared in full size, adult and capable of procreation, so their kind would flourish. It was all such a *wonder*.

Studies today confirm the appearance of different living species at stages, seldom, if ever, over a gradual period but at once. Roy continued to experiment with the plants and animals, making adjustments, some disappeared as new ones arrived, all was needed to make Terra ready for humans. The essential common code was functioning with adjustments made to yield different kinds, each of their own nature and never to be replicated except as part of their own via reproduction.

Terra was as a canvas on which a new creation was being painted, with overlays as needed to obtain the desired result.

Excess greenhouse gas removal added to the resources, such as coal, natural gas, oil, limestone, marble, gypsum, phosphates, and sand, all essential for human civilization. Humans would be part of the animal kingdom but uniquely different, and distinctively human.

Between Terra 1.8M and Terra 500T a creature with human-like features appeared—Homo erectus. This was not human. Close possibly, but not the correct, perfect, final design; more of a trial than a precursor, lacking essential components, intellectually deficient, and to eventually become extinct. This hominid was not a transitional human life-form, it was separate and distinct.

It took more time, and, around Terra 50T, the DNA for man and woman was ready. Terra was a rare planet, the most rare, in fact the only one that was ready to deal with the pinnacle of complex life, the delicate balance of needs prepared for Roy's ultimate objective. Terra was ready for human existence.

"You have done your jobs well," said Roy as he spoke with the gathered Ontologics. The oneness of Roy, a pneuma of his essence, and his image as human was shown in depictions of this revelation. His functionary components, all three, were succeeding. He would continue to speak of what *we* accomplished and the result of *our* accomplishments. The next stage would be to have *our* image made in human form.

Readiness of Terra for humans and the human formula—DNA—thus humans, both occurred at once. Wonders upon wonders continued. The right stuff, the critical code, the true essence was ready. Everything designed, engineered, and made, prior to the advent of a human, was a step in the time continuum to forming man. Each step was necessary for the next.

A supernatural essence was at work forming needed physical elements. All elements were physical, the sun, the moon, stars, water, land, plants and trees, each arriving at their proper time in the one dimensional time continuum as humans know it, then came the fish and the animals, all before man.

Inherent in man would be something different, not just physical but supernatural, too, a combination of the elements of Terra, relationships critical, the physical nature of the planet, but now also Roy would find a place in the nature of humans formed.

The basic template had been present on Terra for millions of years. Roy wrote a language, as it were, a formula, his intellect engaged, his efforts to date studied, and then imbued this formula with the final piece, a small percentage but the most significant element, that of conscious thought and intellectual capacity similar, but falling just short, of his own. It was a mechanism to fuse together two realms—that of Roy's infinite dimension and that of Terra's finite dimension.

It was the final puzzle piece. The table contained many pieces aligned and connected but needed this final key. It was as if the battery to a Lego composite was installed, the plus and minus indicators in correctly, and a switch to *on* brought everything to life.

Roy would have man on Terra. Designed into the human model was the mechanics of thought. Reason could be applied to Terra and Roy's *being, essence,* and *nature* would be made known. Roy's *revelation* would be *human's contemplation.* Roy intended man to rely on this gift of logos and not on Roy's *revelation* alone. It was through logos applied that a relationship with Roy would be possible and *his revelation* would become obvious. Engaged in learning, knowing, growing, and becoming wise humans could know Roy. The part that human's would play in Roy's engineering would be evident and the scenes of the many acts to transpire would fall into place. As there was much turmoil in the advent of Terra, for man there would be much turmoil in life. That turmoil would continue until Roy's ultimate redemptive revelation would happen.

Roy established a well supplied, beautiful, orderly, and verdant garden—a terrarium. It was paradise. Separated from all other areas on Terra, paradise was surrounded by a large wall. The perimeter wall defined and limited the occupants to the confines of the garden. The garden expanse was huge, and seldom were the surrounding walls even visible. The garden was more than adequately supplied with life-supporting nutrients. Filled with flowers of many kinds that constantly bloomed and provided a variety and harmony of colors and pleasing aromas, it provided pathways to stroll, frolic along, and enjoy. There was more than adequate shelter and places to sleep. There were pools of azure blue water that allowed for occasional dips along with joyful splashing and play. There was no meaning to embarrassment. It was safe and secure. It was *paradise*. It was an example of Roy's dimension now on Terra.

A mist rose from Terra to water plants, shrubs, and trees. A river flowed through the core and divided into more rivers. There was no rain, but everything was more than adequately fed with Roy's water. Sufficient food was provided. All that grew were pleasing to the eye. There were multiple types of trees in the garden. They were elegant, fruit bearing, and shade providing. One variety had a special taste; it was sweet and provided energy. Roy's purpose for this attractive, well-shaped, verdant green and inviting tree was medicinal. It was to provide longevity, a life eternal, and no death to the humans. Animals were also in abundance, to include cows, birds, and fish in the rivers.

A-man with Y-chromosomes was introduced into the readied Terra paradise garden. Roy used his own image as the template. Equipped with eyes to see, hands to touch, skin to feel, a nose to smell, ears to hear, and a tongue to taste, the human would have the ability to take-in Terra as no other. Added to the body of man was a soul, visible, and invisible.

This man was to tend the garden and care for the beasts. Man was instructed on what to do, and what not to do. While A-man strolled the area he would name the beasts. But it was not good that A-man be alone. He needed a helper. To help maintain the area and generate the species, A-man needed a woman. Thus from A-man, E-woman with mtDNA was produced. The first man and woman were made physically and spiritually alive— alive with Roy's pneuma. Roy had dominion over them; man was given dominion over Terra—to multiply, fill, and subdue Terra.

Everything the *engineer* worked on, modified, developed, and eliminated—the entire process—stopped at the DNA moment when coded humans—the thinking, conscious, discerning, and compassionate humans—arrived. The brain and mind of man was the last piece of the puzzle for the DNA-coded formula of man. The human brain was and remains the most complex physical object in the cosmos.

The conscious self that is man is only of Roy's doing. Having intellect and dexterity, man was made unique. The ability to communicate is the critical distinction of humans from other animals. Nothing like the human had ever been present prior. It was for Roy the most exciting moment of his adventure in design and engineering. Man was equipped as a rational being able to observe Roy's revelation, understand, and apply logic and reason to cause and effect within the framework of that which had been revealed.

Roy used parts of what he learned along the way, but modified much of his formulas before the final product was brought to Terra. At the same time, Terra was fully ready for the human that appeared. It may not have been the best possible world, but for Roy it was the best way for humans to make it to be the best world. The essentials were in place, with tolerances so close, plant relationships so specific, natural laws well established, Terra's temperature within proper ranges, greenhouse gases in perfect harmony, needed food stuffs available, animals present to aid man in his work and his personal needs, birds to sing and to fertilize, fish to provide food as well; everything was finished.

It was an anthropic *wonder*.

All the dials in the control room were set in their optimum position. The laws of nature were derived from the concepts of divine law, divinely inspired. It was good. Yom six ended.

ooooo

The *engineer* then rested.

The Ontologics came together in preparation for a celebration congratulating Roy.

"You have exceeded our expectations," they said and partied.

"Our work is not done," Roy reminded them.

"Now we have a human who will be engaged in the process. They will have a central role to play," he said.

"And that is?" the Ontologics asked.

"You will see."

ooooo

No more new plants and animals; it was just man. And man would know Roy; their heart would know Roy. Roy made humans that way. Extinct life-forms were not replaced. Everything else was stopped—no longer necessary. It was now up to man.

Everything in the evolving cosmos and Terra was done for the human.

Salt levels of the sea and man's blood stream were adjusted to a level of 3.4 percent. A fraction one way or another and man would not live. Hydrogen and oxygen levels were made exact and just a thousandth of a degree in either direction or man could not survive. The tilt of Terra, 23.5 degrees, and the gravitational force of the moon, made it possible for humans to fill Terra. The distance from the sun to Terra was just right, 93 million miles; a few miles in either direction or the earth would be too hot or too cold for human existence. All the monitors reflected adjustments to the exact tolerances; so many critical relationships were established, tested and proven effective for the strain of humans to come into being. Man. Into man Roy breathed life.

The bombardments, the moon, the deposits from the comets and the asteroids, the early life-forms, the middle life-forms, and the later life-forms, the plant history especially the plant deposits and decay, and the production of fossil fuels were all part of the concoction the *engineer* required to enable his image to be put in action in the form of *man*. Oxygen was a most essential component. There was no transition from one species to another to form man, and no such records can ever be found, as Roy made man in his image when Roy, the *engineer* that he is, felt the time was right. Man simply appeared, unique, well engineered, and ready to take on Terra's future challenges, at the same time caring for self and fellow humans.

So much careful planning was required and the time needed unbelievable. It was all purposeful and for a purpose.

Man is not a product of the primordial ooze of the cosmos or swamp slime on Terra. Man is the product of Roy's handiwork alone.

The anthropic principle that all on Terra was and is for the purpose of sustaining the life of humans came to be. The *engineer* rested at the point he made *man*, placing *man* in charge of what was available for his needs.

Terra provided everything man needed to discover and know his environment, his history, his animals, plants, and companions. Many animals that came before man have become extinct, no longer needed. Man exceeded in ability that of any Neanderthal or hominid as they had become extinct. What remains is what man continues to require. The culmination of Roy's purposeful engineering was human beings. Thanks be to Roy.

In the paradise garden, A-man and E-woman would live forever. Roy's functionary as sustainer was with them. They were alive physically, spiritually, and eternally.

The Celebration

Roy was the cause of it all, the first cause, from his dimension apart from space and time—a dimension he may allow us to know in his own time. If there was a *buck* to stop, Roy was the stopping location. It was from his breath that Terra was formed and spoken into existence, he commanded; and it came to be and stood firm. He wrote the laws that make the whole world function. His realm where all was begun and, after the Terra we know can no longer support human existence, will be where all will continue and where Roy can return.

Roy's presence is everywhere on Terra and in the cosmos, from the sparkling, glimmering stars at night dotted by a pronounced *moon*, at times full, and at times a crescent. His presence shimmers from fallen rain coating plants and grass, filling streams and replenishing fresh water sources. His presence is known from the sound of a baby's cry to the wrinkled smiling face of a ninety-year-old, from the first snowfall to tulips, from puppy dogs to elephants, from the smell of spring and the color of a rainbow, to your imagination and dreams, it is Roy on duty.

Roy stopped just about everything, so it would appear, once Terra and humans were together. There was the need for a period of reflection. It was time to gather his fifth dimension team and celebrate. So much had been done.

"You have done well. The setting for the grand party is complete. We can now begin to serve the humans. Let us join together and praise our good intentions. My thanks to you."

Roy was relaxed, pleased, and respectful of the accomplishments. He was mindful of the roles his associates played.

All the work to date served the objective Roy desired and so much good work had been accomplished. For seven days, Roy reviewed each step of the process, each Yom, and for each he proclaimed and reflected on its success. He was at that point at which all systems were a go. Roy could now rest among his life-forms, take up residence within the space continuum he engineered, and observe the support systems in operation. He had his dwelling place as well as the humans, man and woman, with whom he could share his grace, the glory of his deed, and his love. He, his team, had achieved much. It was an inaugural event. It was Yom seven.

ooooo

The transition, from another dimension where Roy and his associates were somewhat enslaved in a vacuum to a cosmos, a new order, a cosmos upon which Roy could rest in his throne room, resulted. It was all good.

Continuing with his speech to his eternal spirits, his co-hosts, Roy noted, "You have all been most worthy."

Roy was in a position now, at the helm, at the controls of Terra and its cosmos. The seven yoms were a summation of the wonders of Roy's processes and the seventh yom was when he assumed his seat in the house Roy built.

The seven meant it was finished—complete.

Yet it would continue, there would be more new things, growth of knowledge and understanding, and Roy's humans would gain in wisdom, become discerning, know the truth, be set free, and become, most importantly, the stewards of Terra. Also the cosmos gave Roy the opportunity for a relationship with those in his image, mankind, and not just with the divine angelic elements, auras of the fifth dimension, for which he was eternally the host.

"We must all strive for and work toward the ongoing highest standards of mankind." Appearing now before the Ontologics are appetizers and the main course. "Let the celebration continue. You will be asked to intervene at times with humans to aide the plan, to keep this event going without incident. Let them eat, drink and be merry, but know also who is Roy." This was Roy's command to his co-hosts, the Ontologics.

As the cosmos continues to expand, which Roy has not stopped, the concern that arises is how much time humans and their descendants have in the perfect environment—this terrarium of life support for *man*. It can only be *guesstimated*. Roy knew the beginning. Roy was the beginning. He also must know the end. He was before and will be after. What he created he can destroy. It is his to end. This is his show.

Maybe it will take a million years, possibly a billion, maybe even only thousands, an imponderable, as the Second Theory of Thermodynamics, which man has learned by the abilities Roy provided, informs that the expansion of the cosmos must eventually slow. All will settle down and the end will come to pass.

The sun, warming Terra and the face of man, will not be able to continue producing hydrogen at its current rate to enable the explosive forces needed to heat and brighten Terra as it orbits. Temperatures will fall. As the sun dies, Terra will, also, and man will expire before either disintegrates into space stuff and become a component of the cosmological composition. It is not a case of global warming, but of global cooling.

It is the moral consciousness of the human species that are the root linkages, phantom in nature, that as a force pulls one to another, joined in knowing we have an innate responsibility— one for another. Of all the creatures on Terra, Roy gave only man the knowledge of his ways, the right and wrong of his actions, the ability to recall past events, record developments, consider future events and decide on current events. The human species was an emanation of Roy's essence. Everything was engineered, worked out, in conformity with Roy's will. All other creatures on Terra were useful as man's helpers, which only man was able to tame, teach, and equip for man's purposes.

There is intelligence in the cosmos, a product of Roy's mind, his fine-tuning for life, and the infinite brilliance of the essence behind the mission. Roy allowed the pneuma of his mind to reside inside each human awaiting a trigger igniting it for those that so choose a relationship with Roy, a desire to obey and serve Roy.

From the eternal fifth, however, tranquility was not as one would expect. There would be dark clouds passing over Roy's paradise. There would also arise conflict among his co-hosts.

Roy, Man, Niles, Good and Evil

Roy became enamored with his human. Roy loved every human and wanted them to know him and love him, too. It was to be a mutual loving relationship.

With the exacting position of the sun, moon, and stars, man was able to determine days, weeks, months, and years. Man was able to tell time. There were seasons. It was Roy's input that enabled this. This was a gift from Roy to man.

Man's awareness of Roy was clear.

A close associate of Roy's, from the eternal dimension, was jealous and quite powerful in his own right. Frustrated with the power of Roy, wanting credit for his part in the engineering process, he sought to destroy, as Roy's opposite, the human nature of humans initially as desired and planned. He made moves on humans upsetting and disrupting Roy's plan. As a most beautiful associate of Roy, Niles, as did the Ontologics, had free will. Niles was the first to transgress, to fall from the graces of Roy, establishing a precedent for others to follow. He became a rival force in the cosmos. His countenance changed, his anger and resistance gave him a reddish hue. A protrusion, as the beginning of the antlers of an elk, became visible.

"Roy you must know I do not agree with what you are doing. I want more recognition, a greater role with the humans you engendered."

"Wait. You are my no. 1 messenger. You have been most helpful and now you seem jealous. You want a promotion. Your selfish desire is made evident in your appearance."

Niles objected, "I don't know about jealous; I just want more involvement."

"If you rebuke me, you cannot serve me," Roy responded, "you need to follow my lead."

Niles looked at Roy, raised his eyebrows, and said, "I have my own ideas, my own plans. In fact, I think the humans will find what I offer more appealing than what you provide. I will attack your pneuma that dwells within them."

"Everything that has been established has been done according to the plan I have for humans," said Roy.

"There will be resistance. You'll see," Niles uttered.

Niles was the first to rebel. Niles opening salvo in his battle against Roy took place in Dimension Eternal. One-third of the associates and seraphs joined him. They became gang members doing as Niles commanded. The battles were with seraphs loyal to Roy and humans.

On Terra, Niles started with the first two humans. No time to be lost was his attitude. The majority of the work in forming the cosmos and Terra, and its ability to sustain human life, had come to a close. It was now a matter of dealing with man in his capacity to continue Roy's work on Terra. This fallen associate was a most powerful force. At one time a friend and now no more, he had a falling out with Roy, a disagreement on the purpose for man. He was indifferent to the idealistic cosmos palace Roy engineered; he wanted to be a bigger part of the outcome. Control over the humans was in play. He wanted independence. Niles intensely hated Roy's accomplishment, especially the humans.

Having anyone on Terra worship, know Roy, or even want to get to know Roy was anathema to Niles. Niles took up his own cause—that of destroying humans, attacking the very freedom, the essence, Roy provided his perfected humans—at least modifying their orientation to factors other than Roy. He wanted to be worshipped by man. His gang members, demons alike, were brainwashed to assist in his quest. As a seraph himself, Niles needed humans to enact his evil and devious plans on Terra.

Roy often walked in the garden with his two beings, watching and even speaking to them, especially A-man. He could be heard but not seen, yet they knew his presence. They were able to freely enjoy this special garden for many, many years and appreciate each feature that showed Roy's handiwork. Roy had informed A-man of any limitations within paradise.

Niles was watching and observing too, waiting for his moment. He was patient. Then and there in the garden the associate saw his opportunity to intervene. It was his first chance. A-man and E-woman was his target.

These humans, with soul and heart and a good life, needed to be drawn into a different mindset, he felt. He believed if provided assurances they could do as they pleased. Niles wanted these two to feel they were more like Roy than they could imagine, but also he wanted them to know him—Niles.

"Niles," Roy warned, "don't mess with those in the garden."

Roy had tried to instruct the two to avoid the one central garden element, a single unique variety, a forbidden tree, preferring all others and indeed the medicinal sweet tree. Even though other living creatures died, cells died, for these two the cells would replenish themselves forever and ever as long as the medicinal-life tree was accessed for its antidotal qualities.

In a meeting with A-man, Roy provided a specific caveat, "You are free to eat the fruit from any tree in the garden, except one. You must not eat of the central tree."

He pointed to the verdant, flowering and fruit bearing shade tree.

"For when you eat of it, there will be certain very negative consequences," Roy warned. The fruit on this tree was unique, most appealing, colorful and tempting—yet it was off-limits. The fruit never dropped from the tree. As the flower of this plant, it would, when overripe simply fold back into its stem, into the bud of its birth, remain dormant for a spell, and then form a new, replenished, desirable, but not to be eaten.

The associate convinced them, assured them, no harm would come to them if they picked and consumed the available tempting fruit fully ripened on that taboo tree. They would remain physically alive. Niles assurance was *the lie* that would impact humans as long as they lived if indeed they did as he suggested.

"Go ahead, taste it, enjoy it, you will surely not die," Niles head turned to hide the wry smile he had on his face.

The tree was obvious; it was centered in their garden home. Each day they would pass it and gaze upon it, knowing too it was not to be used in anyway for their needs. Even so, A-man and E-woman were curious, aware of this forbidden tree, its fruit beautiful and appealing.

Knowledge, awareness of right and wrong, good and evil, would ensue, Roy warned and Niles knew if the humans consumed the fruit. It would negatively impact the pneuma of Roy inside these people; the quality of life engendered would end. The outcome from indulging would be embodied in the humans, and any of their offspring, forever. It would be a component of any ensuing DNA of the offspring of a man and woman.

The objective of Niles was to convince the humans that Roy's commands were not that meaningful. The freedom the humans enjoyed could be impacted and used in ways to make Niles more noticeable and important in their lives. Control would be made possible for Niles. They would remain free, but their decisions would be modified. It was just a bite, a little taste, what harm could come. Niles could thus free man and make choice possible, their own choice, freeing man from any hold Roy may have had or intended on man.

"Eat the fruit; you will not die, even if that is what Roy told you."

Niles, now a thorn in Roy's side, was going to free A-man and E-woman from the shackles he felt Roy had on them, as Roy had had at one time on Niles as well. Roy had made known man's responsibility was to Roy. A-man was told by Roy to avoid at his peril the fruit of this forbidden plant. Niles, however, in his way, and as an attack on Roy, wanted man to think the human was an equal and the self was most meaningful.

With this freedom Niles would call out, "choose me, listen to me, I will provide pleasures beyond anything you can imagine on this Terra."

Roy had to respond, telling them any pleasure from the invitations and gift basket of the associate would be short-lived and unfulfilling. What Roy offered was an extension to the Terra existence, without denying the possibility of sharing the throne room of Terra with Roy.

However, A-man and E-woman could not resist.

Niles found E-woman alone, separated from A-man. Disguising himself Niles appeared as a friendly animal in the garden and spoke with her. He pointed to the forbidden tree with its taboo fruit and discussed its attributes, encouraging her to try it, "no harm can come of it."

He succeeded in his taunting and tempting with E-woman; she took a bite.

She ate, she lived, it was good; she wanted to share her new found pleasure with A-man.

Finding A-man, E-woman suggested he too take a bite, "it's not bad."

They thus finally succumbed to the entreaties of Niles, at first E-woman. Indeed they thought Niles innocent and convincing, no harm would result, and together they tried the hanging offering on the taboo growth. The humans disobeyed Roy. They suddenly felt odd, a feeling as never before. In all their time in the garden paradise they never felt as they did after consuming the hanging fruit. Their innocence was impacted—poisoned. They felt naked and needed to hide their bodies from each other. Their upright stature was changed as they appeared before each other in a slight stoop. They were embarrassed and ashamed, had feelings as never before. They knew too they were guilty of disobeying Roy. They knew.

The pneuma of Roy, initially present in A-man and E-woman, as a result of their disobedience, went into remission, hidden and dead in the body of the humans.

"You taught A-man and E-woman the secrets of good and evil," Roy screamed at Niles.

"This is just wrong. You are harming those I love. Why? You know I have prepared humans to make good choices. I give them good options. You will always make them unhappy. Look at what you have done! They are now impure, imperfect, their DNA polluted."

It was a seminal moment in the history of humankind.

Niles stared ahead with a wry smile, self-satisfied and feeling success.

"I just gave them more options."

"It was a bad choice. Besides, you told them harm would not come to them. You knew better. The option was not a good one. It was adverse to what I had instructed. You caused them to disobey. You have made them selfish, their flesh weak. For this you must be banned, banished from my council. I know this may be upsetting to you, but for your actions there is no redemption in my house."

"Roy, you will be sorry for this. I will fight you. We'll see who is restored to honor."

"It won't be you, Niles, or those who follow, not without me. You have fallen. You have erred. I made you most-powerful. You know I know you and will deal with you."

"Let's see what happens," Niles spoke defiantly.

In forming humans, Roy made them pure and perfect. The freedom Roy provided was used by Niles, he took advantage, to make evil possible, an imperfection arising from Roy's human design—an indirect result of freedom. Roy knew the risks, never suspecting his own associates would betray him. Roy would continue to love his humans, never forcing their loyalty, yet wanting that very thing.

Just and eternal Roy's hand was forced to punish the humans. They became criminals, committed a crime against Roy in their disobedience.

Niles corrupted A-man and E-woman, depriving them of the perfection of good. Human love, in its truest form, was made possible, though, through this negative act as it is by freedom alone that true love and devotion is possible. A wonderful good resulted, but not without consequences.

Physical death did not occur at the moment. The humans were separated from Roy's pneuma, a form of death; physically they would decay and eventually die. Impossible before, but possible now—Niles caused physical death to take place. Not part of Roy's original plan. The question became the concern of a third form of dying, eternal death, separation forever from Roy. Spiritually, as servants of Roy, they also died. Their souls were modified.

If the choice became that of good vs. evil, those that so choose one over the other would be known and allow Roy to separate the humans into their respectful classifications. Those who would then choose to abuse their new freedom would be cast out, the gates to the eternal kingdom closed to them and their eternal life would be spent elsewhere.

Unfortunately no matter the good, even if weighed on a scale, good exceeding evil, Roy's punishment was necessary as no descendant of A-man would be pure.

It would be like separating wheat and weeds. They grow together, but upon the day of the harvest that which is the good, the wheat, is readily distinguished from the bad, the weeds. The weeds are taken and burned. The wheat is used to provide life-sustaining bread. What was *good* would be addressed.

Immediate measures were needed to be taken as a result of this act of disobedience. Roy acted.

The humans must leave the garden. As punishment Roy had to remove them from any possible access to the medicinal, life insuring, tree. A *no trespassing* sign was placed at the entrance to the garden, guards posted, and the two humans were escorted out—never to return. The whole of Terra, however, remained their playground, just the garden was off-limits.

Standing outside, A-man could see the tree. Touching E-woman he said, "We have erred. This is our punishment. That tree was our cure forever. We no longer have access."

Paradise closed.

Wiping a tear, E-woman came close to A-man. "I did not realize." Looking into his eyes, she said, "We must go forth now as one. Our union is more important than before. We can only strive to be as Roy wanted. But there is uncertainty as never before."

Roy and Niles were at odds—the beauty of the humans, their hearts, represented a battleground between these two. This struggle would continue.

The first two humans survived the ordeal and removal from paradise. They knew too they made a mistake, a critical mistake. Roy remained their friend, continued to love them, but Roy knew he would have to deal with humans and find the means to instruct them on how to live. Perfection was no longer.

The two, A-man and E-woman, were fertile and had many offspring. The human population was to grow, and as they grew, they grew also in wisdom. Roy's cleverness is evidenced in the union of A-man and E-woman and the making of children. By allowing them together to produce humans, new people, he was sharing in part his own experience engineering Terra for humans. He was giving man a piece of his own reality. At the same time each offspring inherited the criminal nature Niles caused in the garden paradise.

ooooo

A moment of reflection on paradise. Was expulsion of the first two humans pre-planned? Did Roy know it was to happen? Roy provided a taste of paradise, a reflection of the future—Roy's kingdom—and then took it away as punishment. It was for a new beginning, a life of struggle, growth, learning, suffering, understanding, wanting, and appreciating the wonders Roy made possible. This was to be a painful but useful historical teaching tool—intended or not.

ooooo

Man was to experience mini-engineering, a daily reflection of the new and continuing development of Terra. The love of the family, A-man and E-woman, their love for each other and for their children, was an example of Roy's love for humans. The pain of childbirth was to be a reminder of the suffering involved as a result of paradise lost. Caring for the offspring, nurturing, feeding, teaching, insuring their safety and security, and setting them free would be as Roy nurtured, fed, taught and set humans free.

A-man and E-woman would experience the growth, from infancy to adulthood of their togetherness and see for themselves the outcome of the effort. A primary attentiveness to the needs of the new humans vs. a secondary level of directed care has essential bearing on the outcomes of the offspring.

Man also experienced lust and coveting desires. Man's heart was not always focused on Roy, just as Niles preferred. The failure in the garden, the wrong action taken as a result of *the lie*, caused man's conviction to the tempter's palate of selfish morsels.

Roy never closes his eyes, he constantly watches over those he loves. The recording Roy wants played over and over for the humans, to be etched on their hearts, minds, and souls, is that his first love, a love critical to the truth in preserving mankind until the end-time, is the children of Roy. Those children are the humans and their offspring. The parent-child relationship was the relationship Roy desired humans would have with him—a deep, respectful love.

However, Niles became ever present. His efforts were constant. At every turn he attempted to put scratches in Roy's records.

Those imperfections were to take man to a track of Niles own selection. Niles was a creature of lies; he encouraged lawlessness; he was greedy, wanting, fearsome, and determined. His weapon of mass destruction was *deception*. In many ways, constantly, *the lie* would be repeated, taking different forms but resulting in similar outcomes. The polluted strain of humans was adept at preferring *the lie* to the obedience toward Roy. Niles was empowered.

Any interruption in the conception of an offspring was a lost opportunity to know Roy. It would happen, but to do so intentionally was problematic. It was murder. It was for Roy a man who cast an obstacle, an unfortunate opportunity for denial and possible avoidance of an experiential session with the one who would love humans as no other. It was a choice of E-woman, but for Roy a wrong choice.

Niles managed to corrupt the offspring of A-man and E-woman. This was upsetting to Roy.

Roy confronted Niles, "I will purge those you corrupt from this human population. Floods, fire, Terra-quakes and other disasters are well within my control."

"Yes," Niles glibly replied, "but many of your loved humans might perish as well. Collateral damage. And once corrupted, always corrupted"

"What I do will always be for the benefit of all mankind. You brought pain and suffering and with it, though, will come joy. It will be the joy of knowing my saving grace as opposed to your destructive poisonous inducements. I will always satisfy. You will leave them thirsty."

"We have our differences, I know," said Niles.

"What if I repent, show remorse for what I have done?" he asked.

"It does not matter," Roy noted.

"You or any of those fallen seraph comrades cannot be restored to prior positions. You are not allowed to return to your former status."

"Then I will fight you Roy," said Niles standing his ground.

"I will do battle with you and take my place by force, if necessary. There are others with whom you are displeased. They will be offered a position as my apprentices."

"I assure you, Niles, I will place in bondage all fallen associates until the Day of Judgment for all arrives. A special place awaits you, an abyss, a prison in which I will watch you squirm," Roy said.

"Yes, but their evil spirits will accompany me, regardless of what you do. We will all harass mankind. We will seek out human bodies to inhabit. You'll see. The male spirits will be malevolent. The female spirits will be seductive" Niles said.

He continued, "Tame them if you can, Roy. Teach them your ways. We will mix with humans and cause chaos. You'll see. Be forewarned. As long as you allow me to reign on Terra, I will rule."

"Niles, you know that in the end you can never defeat me. You may still be serving me, unbeknownst to you, and helping to achieve my purpose, no matter the disruption you cause. My dimension, my realm, will be forever. You will never have the same. Those who follow you will be faced with the burning fire of my wrath. Tell them that and see if they continue to accept your promises."

"Humans will worship the idols I place before them," Niles said.

"Each of your idols will have demonic influences, those of your evil mind and hand, those of your evil band of spirits. I will prevail in sharing the good news. Beware. You may blind the eyes of man to the facts at times. I will share the light of Terra so they will know the real truth. Those that know me will know the difference. They will see. I will always be ready to accept a repenting human," Roy said.

"Roy, your humans are ignorant. I will prove it. Their imaginations are vain. I will use them. The candy I offer is more to their liking than your water. I will harden their hearts so they will never accept what you proclaim. You will be a myth."

"Then know this," Roy staunchly answered.

"I am ready to do battle. In the *end* you cannot possibly be victorious."

The *mastermind* of the powers of darkness, deception, and evil was born in the fallen seraph associate, Niles.

"I will say to everyone, "Roy continued, "You, who deny my right hand, depart from me. You will be cursed and face everlasting fire. I will prepare such a blast-furnace for you, Niles and your evil spirits, and all who follow you."

The *great soul* of the eternal dimension was now at war with the *mastermind* of the powers of darkness, deception, and evil.

ooooo

The *bad news* is man was made forever a criminal; *the lie* spoken in paradise was corrosive and caused Roy's pneuma in humans at that time to decay and die. Man would do terrible things. Man would struggle with life, with love, with happiness, with acceptance, and with security. Man would have doubts, question his purpose, and his existence. Man disobeyed Roy and lost everything.

Roy was true to his word—his punishment immediate. All will not be saved. Every corrupt act of man will be punished. Death will never be reversed on Terra—no matter the medical advances achieved. The pneuma of Roy dead in man, in remission at best, allows for a vast variety of crimes, in thought, word, and deed, all punishable by Roy, not necessarily by man. There would by Roy's demands and man's demands for humans. This is the truth of the *bad news*.

Know this that the humans are incapable of correcting the flaw of man caused by *the lie* of Niles and man's disobedience toward Roy, not on their own anyway. Help would be needed. Man would need to come to grips with the fact that being a slave to *the lie* and serving Roy at the same time was not possible.

Humans—
Outside of Paradise

Paradise was Lost. Humans remained. Roy would be with them even though much had changed. Their purity of spirit and perfect nature was corrupted.

Mumbling among themselves the Ontologics were saying, "What becomes of A-man and E-woman now. They are altered, changed from Roy's initial plan."

Overheard, as Roy hears everything, Roy spoke up, "Paradise is the example of what is possible for man. It was a taste of the eternal realm of our dimension on Terra. Their failure, whether planned or not, which you can speculate about, was not all that was considered for humans. The facts of paradise will be known from here forward and remind mankind of what was. Now all other facets of life on Terra will unfold."

Outside the gates of paradise, children were born. Combining the DNA from man and woman continued the strain, each new form unique and wonderful. Each human system containing also a glue, an element vital for the maintenance and survival of tissues, but also a clue to Roy's presence and saving nature. In him all things would hold together, a laminate protecting the structure. Propagating a world population with humans, the code uniquely and mysteriously reproducible, was now in play. Roy remained in the picture; his functionary ever present.

Man would be a useful and the needed element for Terra's operation. As one man's term on Terra ended others were present to continue the work. Only Roy was required. Roy would have a perfected human being whose life was finite. That perfected being, corrupted in paradise, however, would also have purpose and freedom. Roy's heart would be in his plan for man through all generations. This was an exciting part of the human; with human freedom Roy would have the opportunity to determine those that could be part of his eternal palace—not all would qualify.

The wonder to Terra and all that was for man alone would cause fear—fear of the unknown, not knowing or not fully understanding. The mystery of Terra was *caused* for humans would remain. Questions, concerns, apprehension, doubt would prevail. All this attributed to the mind of man. Man would not rely on Roy's *will* alone. The mystery would be allowed by Roy to be revealed in parts, as necessary. Roy kept his eye on those that feared him, and they that had hope in his unfailing love to be their deliverer would find the joy, the excitement, the promise, discover the gift and their purpose. It would all be revealed to them. The one who trusts will never be dismayed.

Roy provided man access to see into space and see the beginnings of time and space as engineered. The humans were given the skills to determine the code of DNA. In so doing man would realize the mathematical impossibility for chance to result in such a complex formula. Man would know the living machinery to reproduce identical DNA spirals, the process and the importance of the RNA tool with its own complex code, the formation of DNA, could never be a random act.

Random mutations to form intelligent life were not possible. The elapsed span of time since the beginning alone would not provide anything close to an acceptable consideration of such a probability. Roy left nothing to chance. The process was obviously not a random act. If it was, it would have been a cruel hoax on the agents of his work to create chaos in the face of a beautiful living body with a mind and soul and the ability to love the *engineer*.

70

The *engineer* is aware and preparing *man* for the final outcome. Why not? Why would Roy waste this embodiment of the transcendent force he is? We are the *engineer's* life on Terra, deposited in this possibly less than perfect world for his purpose. Might Roy prepare other universes to sustain life?

The *engineer* continues to aid man, thus a reason for storms, hurricanes, tornadoes, Terra-quakes and other disasters humans call natural disasters—even disasters considered evil. These events are good for man as they continue to stir the pot of life-support by supplying needed rain, scattering solar radiation, cooling oceans that become too hot, as well as cooling too hot continental land masses. Yes, there is collateral damage. Such damage is far exceeded by advanced-life productivity. This may seem callous and something Roy could avoid, but not without an even greater cost to his humans.

Changes in soil provide essential nutrients, Terra-quakes a cause. Tectonic activity helps too in compensating for the sun's luminosity. Wildfires burn excess organic litter and allow seeds to properly germinate. Charcoal absorbs chemicals that inhibit plant and microbe formation; dwindling in time and then needing replenishment. Dust and ash can form new wetlands. Lightning produces needed nitrogen. The cycle must be repeated. Roy has his reasons.

The *master* was aware humans would be unique by having an intellect, being smart, and handy. He formed them that way. They could also sing and dance, dine civilly together, paint, sculpt, and write. Man could comprehend his surroundings and appreciate the vision before him. He made man conscious of his environment and his self. Man was imbued with an ability to invent, make, and use tools. Humans were interconnected by the presence of Roy. Like Aspen trees whose root system connects from one tree to another, all Aspens alive as a result of this one massive woven system, an underground labyrinth of ganglia, a mysterious connection to Roy, exists.

Lessons

Multiple generations passed. The *master* sought a *leader*, an example, to demonstrate what he expected of man. Chaos was ongoing. Roy continued to love man; he needed their attention. That one person would be a beacon for other men; his lineage would provide and carry his legacy to many nations on Terra. He would share and instruct in the knowledge of Roy's expectations and provide the historical pathway focused on the good Roy proclaimed man to do. Through him and his offspring Roy would entrust his personal commitment so they might know Roy in ways as no other and use such awareness well till the end.

Niles, at the same time, continued his revolt and path of corrupting influences enjoying a Terra with more that knew his offering than Roy's. The cities that were established did so without respect for one another, without taking actions that supported what was right; it was a *me* culture, paganistic. There were successes in developing architecture, music, literature, even libraries, but the scrolls, the art had a leaning toward immoral practices and activities more acceptable to Niles than Roy.

Terra had enjoyed a run without rain, without disruption, needed water supplied in a humid tropical setting. Devoid of love and finding but one that Roy thought worthy, Roy acted to clean the slate of his engineering, and rid Terra of the damning influences of Niles. He released waters from the firmament above. The springs and caverns of moisture imbedded in Terra gushed forth reshaping the landscape. A flood ended the lives of many

Nile's contemporaries and left Terra with but a few humans. It was an experiment that would change the course of Terra, even its shape, introducing weather and its potentially damaging effects. Roy wanted his pathways followed. He extended his hand and demonstrated his wrath and vengeance.

Following the pathways established by Roy and expressed through few leaders, however, was an everyday decision. Not an easy decision. New humans were born to Terra, all imperfect. Niles was ever-present.

ooooo

Roy's most ardent first *leader* heard Roy, felt his presence, and respected him as a supernatural influence on his life. At a young age, he took his wife and father and left a vibrant city, advanced in its day to include a library with records from the day of the earliest humans, to travel. He was inspired by Roy to go. He settled on a new land. He bore children at an old age. Life, though, was not easy; there was suffering. He, unfortunately, transgressed with the encouragement of his wife, who was considered barren at the time but wanting a son. He had a first male child with another woman—a woman known to the family, a servant to his wife. Some time later his true natural son was born, a significant wonder and surprise for these older parents. Then, jealousy as the cause, the leader's first child, born not of his wife, was cast out of the household.

Roy was able to speak to his friend. The friend could only sense a presence. His head turned from one side to another, seeking the caller. His tunic of reds and tan stripes swayed as he turned searching. He held his turban secure with one hand as he peered about. A resonant tremolo was heard. This first-leader-friend was informed by the functionary of Roy of the external influence on Terra.

"Do as I ask you. Take your son and go where I tell you."

He knew and was compelled to seek Roy having only hope of such an influence. Roy wanted to be certain this friend was aligned with him. There would be a test.

The life of his natural son, the son of the first-leader-friend, was loved dearly by his father. It became a nerve-wracking exercise in knowing the extent to which a loving and loyal father will go for his faith. The leader-friend was commanded by Roy to do unimaginable harm to his heir.

"Prepare a fire for a burnt offering."

He loved Roy so much he may have sensed no matter the pain of the dare Roy would provide, no harm would be done.

The son sensed a terrible outcome, but the father said, "Roy will provide for the offering."

If it was to be death, then so be it. A knife was drawn in preparation when an Ontologic appeared, "Do not lay a hand on that boy!"

In the bramble bushes was a horned animal to be the sacrifice. It was a substitute. Such an act could result from an unknown, never perceived action; after all, it was Roy in control. His love and loyalty were proven; the son's life saved.

Roy had a friend. Roy had confirmation.

This act aided in identifying and establishing this *leader's* lineage as that which would be most useful to Roy. This became the future clan from which Roy's program would be plainly demonstrated. The son would be the first salt of a descendant of great significance.

Both sons of the leader became themselves leaders on Terra, but only the natural son was given the promises of Roy in his heritage. Roy found the DNA strain to continue and carry forward his heritage. His battle with Niles would be won through this biological strain.

Niles was all the time watchful. He had his eyes focused on the child of an adulterous affair.

Roy saw the need for increased leadership and chose specifically a cadre of persons within the line of the natural born son of the first *leader*. These persons were guided by the promises and taught from the stories relayed from generation to generation of Roy's omnipresence and actions. Further action steps would be taken, with stumbles and falls along the way, using these persons as instructors and examples, with guidelines to be passed on to the many that were to follow.

Taking one of the co-hosts, a valued Ontologic aside, Roy informed him, "Mike, as my chief prince you are being assigned to watch over this leader-friend and his seed. His descendants are essential to making known my promise and message to all of mankind. You are now placed in charge of the Ontologics that will defend us against the evil spirits of Niles. Niles and his fallen comrades will continue to make every attempt to resist and thwart our plans."

Mike nodded accepting his heightened position.

No longer active in the inner-sanctum of Roy's realm, Niles had to be kept away, his activities observed and resisted as required. Mike was to be the lookout and defender.

ooooo

There were occasions, few, when Roy actually appeared on Terra, testing the conditions. He knew his presence would scare people so he decided carefully where and when. Wanting his Terra to be well tended and his people in harmony, each visit he imparted knowledge and guidance. He was heard but unseeable.

Roy's concerns were for the preservation of Terra and the education of man until Roy could finish preparation of an even better Terra-realm for those most thankful, most accepting, ready, and most obedient to his requests.

Niles had plans of his own.

The Mind, Education, and Wisdom

Terra was new, newly born, and so too all the elements that comprise the functioning of this planet. Man was new as well and very different, very different from the Ontologics of the fifth dimension Roy always knew. As much understanding as Roy had in the embodiment of man and Terra, there was little understanding by man of Roy. Roy made man in his image, but he did not make man a clone of Roy—man and Roy were not the same. His desire was to have all humans love and appreciate him for what was done for them, while at the same time coming to grips, experiencing and learning what they needed to know and do for Terra and Roy. All of these expectations were present while never really seeing or hearing Roy, but having to simply sense, be taught and be conscious of Roy's existence. This was to be a task unto itself.

Think about having a close personal relationship with friend, or a wife. It has flesh and bone consequences. You can touch, feel, see, and hear. You know when someone is next to you. If you are struck, you may bleed, they may bleed, and certainly you feel contact. In air, there is nothing, just stillness, warmth, cold, a breeze, or wind, but there's no potential for a relationship.

You may not see electricity, but shocks are possible. Thus, making known the power, but there's still no potential for a relationship. Without being seen can Roy ever be knowable, or available for a relationship. Roy would find a way. His essence is present in all we experience, the wind, the electricity, the human contact, and all that surrounds. Taste, touch, smell, and see Roy where you stand right now.

The education of man would take time, as did the formation of Terra, and had stages of its own. It would require leadership and guidance.

The existence of man alone in an age-adult form did not assure a wise person capable of dealing with others, Terra or the cosmos. The term *adult* carries with it its own obstacles. Is the age of a person the imperative to defining *adult?* What is that age? Society may make a determination and in turn structure laws and freedoms accordingly, but is the *adult* in society an *adult* cultur-ally—as to development, composition, knowledge and wisdom—the same?

Defining a child not just as a baby, infant, or little boy or girl, but even as an *adult*, an adult not as yet ready to comprehend the world of Terra, then as a child the norm is more that of instinct, intuition, contemplation and simple reactions, judgments made without any foundational experience, and knowledge or know-how. The functioning adult, on the other hand, reacts to inputs and outside influences with a considered response, wise to Terra and mankind, and as a contributor. Teachers were needed and at the start there were principally two—Roy (the good teacher) and Niles (the bad teacher).

As Terra became more populated and conditions on Terra changed, knowledge of the workings of Terra and others devel-oped. Allowance for scientific discovery was provided. Roy's chosen leaders helped him teach about the ways he desired and knew as the proper pathway to the future Roy intended. Some of the growing population sought ways to not focus on Roy's hopes for mankind.

There were the persons who continued a life driven by instinct and intuition as well as personal desires (the Nephilim). They were taught by others of like mind and desire, trained in the hab-its and practices of persons who never knew Roy, or possibly had no desire to know Roy. The man without the inner sense of Roy's presence does not have the capacity to understand the things that come from the pneuma (spirit) of Roy; they seem silly, foolish, and not necessary for their lifestyle. He cannot or will not understand them, because they require an inner sense and openness to be discerned. They may have known Niles better.

They did, however, contribute to Terra and mankind, developing cities and music and art, but at the same time pursued pleasures. Oddly enough, sensing the supernatural, they established multiple idols of worship. The animal nature of man, a part of man, was an overriding factor in their lives, a pagan style where virtues existed in different forms in different communities depending on desires, wants, needs and the accomplishments of the more highly visible, prominent persons. There were athletes, scholars, philosophers, politicians and others which having achieved a level of respect (at least the respect of their community and as an example of the primary activity of the community) who became symbols of virtue—whether rightly or wrongly. Niles had his influence. Roy's hand remained in their accomplishments regardless of the fact they did not comprehend Roy.

The mind of man, its development and training was to continue—so too the education. From the child-stage to the teen-stage the teaching process changes, responding as needed to the pupil. At the teen-stage instinct and intuition evolves more into wonder. A need for some control over the early learning stages, for each individual and for mankind as a whole, was seen as a necessity by Roy. Niles thought differently. Exposure to facts and influences before the correct time, that moment judged by Terra's elders, could disrupt the appropriate flow of inputs and negatively influence understanding as the mind may not be developed to the level needed to properly interpret the inputs as right or wrong. Like the grapes in a fine wine, if picked before their time the wine may not be as great, or as expected—the outcome unpredictable or disappointing.

The philosophy of existence was a matter for daily contemplation. Rivers and streams flowed to their outlets every day, a never ending supply. Periods of drought suggested change to be followed by recovery and rain, the streams and rivers having the same source and outlets as before. The seasons repeated, summer, fall, winter, spring. Man's toils were productive but the answers may not be there, satisfaction elusive even when great structures, houses, gardens, orchards, water pools, sacred places and prized designs came from the hand of man. Was everything meaningless? Roy would insure that was not the case.

Pleasures in abundance, beguiled by the wine and beauty of living, held for a moment until sought anew. Rewards of gold, silver, and other resplendent treasures may be accumulated, but to what end. Music, singing, dancing, and the merriment of the party lasted till the tune and time ended. Like the wind, it blows, but then abates, to possibly blow again in a new direction. Was it folly? Was it meaningless? Was it vanity? What is accomplished? Little or nothing? Where was the joy? Thoughts of existence, a short stay on Terra as the dash between birth and death dates on a tombstone, sought the looking glass key, the search function. There was reflection; there was a request for *meaning*. Upon death, wealth goes to what end—to a non-productive relative, or to one who is deserving or not? Will there be benefits, gratefulness, or dependence and idleness resulting from a productive life passed on? Who will remember the generation prior? Your parents may be close, but their parents and parents' parents, and parents' parents' parents, and so on, called grand and even more grand, are they remembered? Is their lot and toil in life of any consequence? Man's relevance is in question by man. What is purposed in each life, in a presence on Terra, and in the *who am I?*

Man would always have an inner sense of a supernatural influence on man and Terra beyond man's control (manifested in multiple gods or Roy or Niles), but would constantly need to seek clarity to know and remain on the correct path. Asking Roy was an option, if they knew Roy, had faith in Roy, or contained within them the inner-sense, the functionary, which is Roy.

The educated man, by Roy's design, would grow and from his surroundings learn, also from his elders learn, and from his teachers learn, receiving a balanced diet of knowledge so better to make proper decisions in the adult-stage. Maintaining a balance in the forum of learning would always be a challenge. Wisdom is attainable.

There were leaders that made known Roy's presence to others and his role in Terra. Those who listened, who were taught by them and followed, were then equipped to carry this message forward so others too could have understanding and wisdom.

The ethical and moral standards of Terra was put in place by Roy, but needed to be incorporated into man's nature through the education process. In part a natural instinct, but in reality enhanced as a learned fact. What is obvious was the good in humanity was wired into man's DNA. The bad in humanity came from free will; it too was a component of man's DNA.

The final stage of education, the utopia, may not be fully attainable or immediate, but it has its own beginnings, likened to a second birth or a rebirth.

The onset of the adult-stage is when the instinct and intuition of the child-stage and the wonder of the teen-stage result in knowing; when the apprentice becomes the teacher or master and is able to then continue to grow and even develop unimpeded; when the human can make improvements independently, while at the same time taking responsibility and aiding in the on-going education of those in the child-stage and teen-stage, and even a pre-adult-stage; when attained is a level demonstrating wisdom and the culmination of the foundations of essential education. This rebirth, when the adult emerges along with knowing, is the advent of wisdom.

As with man Terra is also learning, continuing to emerge as the whole of mankind gains in experiencing the wonders of Roy and the daily reflections of his handiwork. The individual's education is at the microlevel and that of Terra is at the macrolevel, consisting of the years of individual development which over time accumulates and provides greater wisdom as to the relationship between man, Terra and Roy. In addition, in part child, in part teen, in part adult, Terra offers itself to further research and exploration. The outcome of further study by the individual adults within the framework of humanity enables the glories of Roy to be more completely revealed.

With wisdom, the world of Terra can continue as Roy intended. As part or all of Terra achieves the level of wisdom to which Roy hopes, Roy's eternal dimension will be visualized. The more that see his eternal realm, the more there will be harmony and evidence of Roy's grace and peace as well. Roy is open to all who see his light shining on their persons. He is most amenable to all who embrace his engineering and welcomes them into his fold.

On Terra what may escape many humans is the command by Roy given to subdue all of Terra and its contents. Inherent in that order is toil, the expenditure of human energy to maintain Terra, its species, its trees and flowers, its water and food supply, and all that comprises life and living. It would be a repetitious process to the end. Knowing Roy and making the effort is the blessing and purpose for each human. Man's labor is significant. Lack of joy in his labor may demonstrate ignorance of Roy's plan. With no joy in work comes depression, emptiness, and a sense of futility. Know that Roy has made a time for everything—to include injustice and oppression. Without Roy in the life of a human, enjoyment would be elusive, just as chasing the wind.

Roy may have had a concern that at the point human progress, wisdom and knowledge became significant, the engineering may have been too perfect, and some humans may consider themselves like Roy. Niles lurks in the crevices prepared to remind humans of such a possibility. The cause of such an outcome may be confusion and doubt as to Roy's direct influence. Beware of premature inputs provided in the early education stages that misdirect the pupil.

The curriculum to be taught and the timing of teaching basic skills, subjects, ideas, and philosophy are critical. The question will always arise as to content and when pupils are being indoctrinated into a specific cultural idea, as opposed to learning practical knowledge, ethical and moral values, and foundational imperatives that will enable future decisions based on wisdom. That was a risk, but the importance of man being inventive, curious, creative, and productive, as well as aping (imitating) Roy, was flattering and welcomed.

Niles though would always be present and have his say whenever possible. He knew well the flawed, joyless, and hopeless man that each human vessel contained. It would be the adult-stage individuals whose education hopefully was guided by persons considered wise, practical, balanced, worthy, and without bias, which would prepare the educational course for the developing humans. Roy's blessings would follow.

Niles's focus became that of the earliest stage of education—the child and the teen, where his charm could be peddled most efficiently. Niles also relied on habituates to entice, capture and control, as necessary, loving the dependency caused.

Order, Consciousness, Freedom, and Concerns

Roy presented his Terra creatures with laws—regulations, with which they could learn, understand, know, and fully utilize his design. Through a *leader*, Roy provided hard evidence, the Tablet Laws, of his basic tenets to share with the people. He duplicated this effort in the family unit where the offspring would be presented with structure and regulations with which they could learn and understand. But once old enough to emerge from the cocoon of home, even prior at times (an early adult-stage), they could rebel, the cause possibly unknown, possibly improper leadership in their training, or simply a show of independence—a freedom of consciousness, a desire to prove oneself without aid from neither parent nor Roy.

The emerging butterfly of man was capable of feeling his significance, his competence, his brain engaged to propel him into an adult social system. It was a reflection on the system of education, for good or for bad. Self-motivation became the stepping stone to a happy, aware, purposeful future, a future in which knowing Roy could have great importance.

Self-motivation is prompted by a person discerning the need to accomplish with the help of a master, to learn with enthusiasm and purpose, to doubt and question, to seek clarification, and to not expect the social order to care for them indefinitely. The self-motivated having a sense of purpose would realize it is not a right to be part of Terra but a privilege, sensing a guiding pneuma within, and to achieve and contribute. There would be joy in toil. With honor and respect for the environment enabled for the life of man, the self-motivated would be thankful, ambitious and strive to attain self-worth.

Reliance on the gifts of Roy and not the expectation of handouts would be a calling. It would be their desire to be dependent and accepting of what Roy provides. Always with a sense of humility, in the adult-stage, the self-motivated would desire ongoing learning, while at the same time being inventive, enthused, and purposeful in serving humanity in return for what humanity provided. The child-then-adult would, with love and proper instruction, conceivably respond well, in a manner characteristic of the organizers—A-man, E-woman, the leaders/teachers, and Roy.

With each generation, the collective knowledge of the world would increase, new discoveries would be made, more choices would be possible, accommodations for a more densely populated Terra would be needed, progress would be ongoing, and the grand multi-dimensional picture of Roy's *wonders* would become more clear. The rules learned would be respected, but they would be tested too. The nature of man is imperfect; the character of man flawed.

No matter the magnitude of instruction—by word, by mouth or by picture, man's freedoms, the choices, would pull and push in varying directions—toward good, toward evil, and then back. Back and forth until at some stage a more stable nature is harvested—with the possibility of good or bad. No matter the child, however, when they become themselves a parent (possibly an adult as well), from an overwhelming sense of love, an experience wherein they now know what true love is actually, the immediate focus is Roy-like.

When first gazed upon the face of Roy is in each child's face. All of life to that point, all wisdom and revelation is Roy, if for only a brief time, and it is good. Roy's hope is that it lasts until he calls, and he has a need, a need for those that believe in him. The children will know about Roy and should be told and taught to develop in the wisdom of achieving a life in the eternal dimension.

Roy enabled man to build schools and hospitals, to preserve precious historical documents and history, to form libraries, build cities and societies, provide benefits for the sick and poor, and so much more. Charity was more apparent in Roy's human model than in Nile's human model. It was Roy's people that accomplished much, preserved much, and did much for all mankind. He poured the foundation for learning.

In addition, man was able to exist on their own. Roy never expected the laws established might someday be used in ways to deny the possibility Terra was designed or engineered, or that the regulations established were by a party from the eternal dimension, other than that of Roy himself. Reliance in future discovery on only that which was present on Terra at the time of study, natural laws, was not anticipated. Some element of the *wonders* of Roy were expected in considerations, research, studies, and outcomes. Roy wanted man to discover without restriction all that was humanly possible about Terra and the cosmos. Roy also anticipated man would see his hand in the mix.

It was the mind and soul of the human, the brain that would always remain as the albatross, and the conundrum of science. Once science attempted to go beyond the study of the nature of Terra to be in and of itself a philosophy, Roy's roadblock, his detour to reality, would be the human mind—mind over matter. The soul of man was also an imponderable.

The distinguishing characteristic unique to humans, the mind, impossible to put a number to, to develop an equation for, or to have resulted, developed by all that is nature, all that is natural on Terra could not be without the brain implanted in the human cranium designed by and imparted by Roy. Thoughts of thought would remain a mathematical equation without a solution. Yes, there were brains in other animals, but none with the ability to think as humans do. For those who see life as empty and repetitious they see man's death as that of an animal, both returning to the dust of Terra. Little are they cognizant of the soul Roy molds for eternity. The human brain is as capable of seeing nothing as embracing something. What may be the contents of a simple toy ball are seen differently by a mind of wonder and joy. The air within may be much more, as a cosmos unto itself.

That was Roy's *Ahah!* moment for all mankind. No rational consideration, decision, or expression could be made in the absence of thought. This was Roy's most precious, most essential, and most important aspect of humans. It was Roy's essence. The brain is the physical, temporal piece of the human, but its contents, the mechanics, the capabilities and the miracle of it are all a piece of Roy. Inside is the spiritual grab bar that can pull man from despair to joy.

His own exclamation, when man uttered his first word, expressed his first thought, embraced another human, and considered consequences of acts committed or to be committed was, "Yes! That is precisely what I want."

Roy found ways to inform humans and record inputs he supernaturally provided for all mankind. All the information provided was handed down over long Terra periods; and when written, Roy insured his purpose and instructions for man were made clear. Hidden in the treasure of what the humans wrote were revelations of the past, present, and future of Roy's work. Those treasures were there to add to knowledge and wisdom. It was to be Roy's legacy. Stepping out of nothingness and into reality was revealed and noted. Roy also provided instruction for his humans. Much of the guidance dealt with resisting overtures from Niles. He gave them lists of items to properly observe so one human can get along with another. Knowing the conscious mind of man Roy made inherent that which is correct and that which is in error when considering actions to be taken.

Roy engineered man with a piece of himself inside. Man errs and knows his errors, some decidedly worse than others, especially as they apply to other humans. Animals, all those that came before man (and none, as a new species, have come since) make no conscious errors. It is only man so equipped with ethics and moral standards as set forth by Roy. Internally present in Roy's human model was a strain of kindness, much more than evil, an internal orientation toward good. At the same time, Roy knew his humans would always consider in one way or another Roy himself, the producer of the staging, the scenery and the play to be enacted on Terra. They could only imagine, but imagine they would.

ooooo

Niles knew what Roy can do and did. He saw an opportunity with the mind of man. He teased and toyed with it just as he did with E-woman in the garden of paradise. The disruption to Roy's plan by Niles caused Roy to address humans and instruct them more forcefully so they were well aware of his fallen comrade. Niles was ever present, ever the tempter of A-man, E-woman, the leaders, the chosen, and their offspring. He started as early as possible in the development stages of a child, taking advantage whenever either parent turned away, their attention diverted to self or other Niles's morsels of desire, their focus distorted, their responsibilities distracted, and the protective parental shield, the defense mechanism Roy himself wired into the mental frame-work of the human, pierced. Niles had help.

Niles is aided by those more oriented toward themselves than toward Roy. Humans were assistants to Niles, knowingly or not. Niles makes the effort to impart his influence as early as possible, at the child-stage if his helpers can assist—even the teen or pre-adult-stage. He was instrumental in forming within societies his own societies. Later stages when the individual is free of parental influence often represent the best chance for Niles to jump in and entice, the person most susceptible to proving his independence without oversight and exposing weaknesses or strengths. He would make those most adverse to Roy's truth, his leaders.

Niles uses man by enticing him with pleasures, with everyday temptations, with a constant din of invitations to transgress, causing whenever possible disruptions to Roy's end goal. Nile's objective was to provide humans a sense of empowerment, the ability to do as they please, even to use Roy as a shield hiding their personal goals, objectives, wanton desires, and control. Seeking credibility, justification, vocal support, and acceptance for ways not those of Roy was to find its way into civilization and find a groundswell of support. Niles was as the red cape that human bulls charge to seek victory over what might lie behind the cloth. Success may not have the consequences or provide the satisfaction initially thought.

Roy provided the pathways to follow to resist Niles's kisses or those of fellow humans encamped along with Niles in the desert of desperation. The desert of desperation was for them an oasis, an apparition of pleasures. Roy managed to provide the methods for man to know, understand, and to find favor from Roy enabling those selected to be with Roy when all came to an end.

For humans, love and ecstatic joy was accompanied by suffering and excruciating pain. It would not be easy, as what Roy had done to make life on Terra possible post-Paradise contained many obstacles. The obstacles arose, as hurdles on a track, when the fruit of the taboo tree was eaten. Sacrifices would be required. Resistance to the bowls of sweetened fruit and candy presented morning, noon, and night by the hand of Niles was demanded.

Food and drink provided by Roy was all that man would need. The properly educated and wise would know. It would take commitment. It was a complication involving the *master* more directly with humans than he may have originally intended. Roy provided markers of where the ultimate authority lies.

ooooo

Thousands of years passed and the human population grew. Nephilim—pagans—followers of Roy's fallen comrade came and went. Roy viewed those that followed Niles as living in the dark. He did what he could to rid his new dominion of nihilistic, empty, ungrateful humans, often doing battle with his comrade, showing his light, but not always achieving the success he wanted. Roy loved even those in darkness, his lighted path always there for those who decided to take it.

Roy provided man with a powerful flashlight to illuminate his way as needed, but at the same time Niles was often present with his hand making every effort to cover the lens, to diffuse or block out the light, to create darkness, and making man trip or take the wrong turn, guided by Niles foot or hand.

Roy had to establish boundaries for man and set many programs into motion. He made it possible for humans to just believe in Roy and they would then have the opportunity to continue on with Roy and his plans beyond the end-time. They would know his requirements and patiently apply themselves to Roy's standards in the hope they would find his favor. Roy's leaders and teachers would relate his messages. Roy reminded humans that while on Terra their role and their job was to follow Roy's outline. Roy was to be their center, their soul infused with Roy's grace. He informed any who would listen that man, his know-how, would establish Terra societies and have senates formed to establish civil rules for a common purpose to engender order. These were man's laws and to be obeyed.

Roy's law, however, was never to be disregarded, not if the way to the time after the end was to be enjoyed with him. It was as if Roy continued calling out to mankind, "I am the first cause and the final cause. For you there is a destination, it is through me you can get there."

The human population grew. There were souls who were disobedient to Roy. Roy decided to meet with the Council of Ontologics. They were anxious to know of Roy's next step. He told them, "We must select among humans a group of people to educate in the positive ways of our domain. We already have leaders and a family in the lineage of the proper DNA strain. Further attention must be given the family, their closest friends as well, as a demonstration group for all other humans." This defined group became known as the people-of-Roy.

In reply, "But they already exist in the extended family, do they not? Those with the DNA strain from the first-leader-friend. Those you promised."

"Yes," said Roy.

"We must guide that group attentively and carefully. They will be our teaching tool."

To the surprise of one individual in the people-of-Roy, a leader was selected. Dubious at first as to his being picked, Roy confronted him with instructions for leading a segment of the existing population—those that held the promises given the son of the first-leader-friend. Relying on the promises of Roy, they remained steadfast to each other, clinging often however to idols of their own making. They followed this selected man for many years. Roy provided food and water. Having found someone Roy knew could lead his people he then provided the Tablet Law, a tangible record of the essentials that were to guide humans toward goodness—the Goodness Navigation Device or GND.

With a display of Roy's eternal realm in action—lightning, thunder, and clouds of smoke—the leader of the people-of-Roy was called away from his flock by Roy. After an extended period of separation, he emerged from the fog walking down a mountainside, his full length robe flowing and waving in the strong winds, his right arm wrapped about the GND. The people noticed a lengthy more white than gray beard grown during the time away. The beard appeared as a scarf wrapped around his neck. He looked taller. He was quite impressive and commanding in stature. He carried the Tablet Law, the GND, for all to observe. What many inherently sensed as right and wrong was now visually real and documented.

In a simple all encompassing form the GND was presented to a large gathering of people-of-Roy. It was the decalogue.

The main issues were to respect and honor Roy, parents, to be truthful, to not lie, and to not steal. Humans were not to take the life of another. Humility and selflessness was noteworthy, captured in a clause that provided a broad *shall not. Covet* was the operative term. In all ways the rights of others were to be regarded, jealousy was to be kept at bay, the property and possessions of others were to be left alone, not revered, and not wantonly desired. Desiring other than Roy was wrong, in whatever form.

For centuries the GND, kept safe in a box, ornately decorated and gilded, was carried on the shoulders of the people-of-Roy as they traveled or went into battle. It symbolized having Roy with them, a constant reminder of the promises of Roy toward those regarded as his own.

The GND as a reminder of Roy was also as a mirror, a reflection of the polluted nature of man, more so than having a sense of right and wrong. The GND made clear the imperfections, the flaws of humans that resulted from The Lie of Niles. It raised the internal thermometer to its upper reaches showing how close to the fiery abyss all humanity stands and the imponderable of being able to serve Roy fully and receive an eternal blessing.

ooooo

Roy's promise was to save man for the new Terra and cosmos only he could provide. Even with obstacles present, mankind was being taught; mankind was learning; mankind was listening; mankind was growing up. Was this all just an experiment, a trial balloon to see if man can obey? The GND made clear what was correct; at the same time, it made difficult the journey. The suffering to achieve the glory of Roy was extensive. History was in the making, but Roy had a dilemma.

There was a concern. The framework for humans, the GND, the legalistic systems, to use to conduct their lives could become an impediment to future growth, knowledge, creativity, and wisdom. Were the gates to the eternal dimension locked, never to be opened as no one could accede to the required standards due to the blemishes on human DNA resulting from hearing and pursuing *the lie*? Those following Roy, the tattooed, were finding it impossible to live in perfect accord with the legalist GND, the Tablet Law, an inspired structure established and transmitted through select elders. Conflict existed among the elders. The elders, many, claimed leadership, knowledge and acted as representatives of Roy. There was confusion. Roy's frustration was demonstrated on many occasions.

Outsiders were invading, allowed by Roy as a lesson, capturing and dispersing the people-of-Roy because of their unwillingness or inability to obey and meet the standards of Roy. Their sanctuary was changing; their numbers spread to many areas of Terra. Roy remained with them, even as dispersed, but sought to improve the nature of the system. The legal framework was restrictive and static. Leaders were interpreting for their own benefit and falsely making claims, not even leading their own lives accordingly.

Before the GND the people of Terra relied on an innate sense of right and wrong, good versus evil, still, however, corrupted by *the lie*. It was clear they sought a supernatural thing as there were many occasions when idols were formed and used to call for weather or crops, or success hunting, or peace from marauding enemies. The GND startled the people-of-Roy into a heightened reality. The mirror of the law reflected on their personal nature, the magnitude, and the all encompassing aspects of habits and lifestyle that were taboo. It made their bad even more bad, their imperfections even worse. No amount of good could overcome the pile of bad that was made inherent by *the lie of Niles* and punishable by Roy.

The standards could not be met, and if only one was ignored, small or large, then all may have been, as each represented a personal affront to Roy. Roy saw a need. The need was for a life focused only on the legalistic foundations which could not be met by anyone. As it was the law, the GND would not allow the people-of-Roy to join Roy in a future Terra. Roy could not allow this to continue. Roy would be closing the door to progress, to a world of future discovery, invention, and growth to satisfy the needs of a growing population on Terra. The standards had meaning, but they became the object, where Roy wanted the people to see him as the object.

A change was needed, a modification, a means to forgive everyone for the mistakes made in meeting the legalistic framework, and understanding their object as Roy. The Tablet Law, the GND, was important. It was an imperative to a life properly led. But it was not to be the final standard for entry past the gates of Roy's dominion. The history of the past would help open eyes to the needs of the cosmos and Roy, providing ethical and moral basics. But a passionate focus on past history could also stop development if obedience to the system became the objective and knowing and having a relationship with Roy became secondary.

It was time.

Dimension-Eternal

There has been discourse on the formation of the cosmos and Terra. There has been discussion on Roy and his associates, the Ontologics, and some mention of the eternal location in which they dwell and from which they function. Niles, an associate and an enemy of Roy, has been presented. There is a need now to know more, understand more, about Roy, the Ontologics, the eternal place, and events taking place.

The area that is the fifth dimension, the eternal arena of Roy, is a concern, worthy of questions. What is it? What is it like? It is not complex or contingent on anything else. In fact making an effort to explain that which has no explanation seems fruitless. For reference we will call this eternal dimension of Roy and his associates *DE* for Dimension-Eternal. DE is everything, has everything, can provide everything, and, for no reason at all, has access to everything. We know it as an eternal; continuous; and a culture consisting of forms, aliens, souls of indescribable proportions and composition.

The forms, Ontologics, or *beings*, as in human terms, are not humans. They may not even contain DNA. The *beings* are entirely distinct and infinitely different from those on Terra, but also immanent. The *beings* on Terra emanate from DE. As their presence everywhere suggests, Roy and the associates exist, if anything exists at all, conditionally without any limitation, and cannot exist. The forms are as seraphs, seraphs uniting as *one*, unifying the souls, as the Logos of all that is known or knowable, as truth and that which is not truth. The seraphs of the Logos serve Roy, an intelligent and most powerful *being*. Collectively they are the counsel in the dominion of DE. The seraphs are celestial attendants of Roy. They cater to him.

Know, though, that within DE events take place as on Terra, often distracting from the happenings, the needs, or the peoples of Terra. As DE may consist of souls, Roy would be the *great soul*. Roy unites the eternal dimension, the seraphs, yet they are not always in harmony. The choir of the voices of the seraphs of DE is mostly beautiful and moving, but at times can be discordant.

All that is in DE is without dimension. DE has no limits. Roy is not constrained by either time or space. No highways or pathways exist. Travel is location dependent with rapid movement possible from one to another, instantaneously. All focus on the chamber in which Roy is housed. Ontologics gather before Roy at his behest. He uses associates to protect believers, to alert believers, to provide revelations, and impart forecasts of future events. This is done to humans on Terra, so they may know what to expect. Some on Terra will hear or see and others will not. Hearing or seeing will depend on their acceptance, love, respect, reverence, and faith in Roy.

Conditions in DE did not change after the process of forming Terra, but the responsibilities of the Ontologics did. They now needed to deal with the humans and Roy's desires with respect to the humans. They had a time and space continuum with which to deal, as a separate arena for football, the Sunday Night event, self contained and unique for its time from the dimension that surrounds. From its beginning, its alpha, until its end, its omega, the Ontologics would be as reporters in the press booth. Roy was their primary audience.

Roy is impossible to describe or explain. His consistency, composition, size or density is an unknown. It is possible for Roy to manifest into a form acceptable to humans. Anything is possible for Roy. This is purposeful so man can relate. If and when a seraph makes an appearance on Terra, a recognizable form will be utilized. If a human were even to gaze upon Roy as he is, they would die. The revelation would be so intense, so overwhelming, they would be consumed by delight. He can be as small as an atom, or less, and as large as Terra, or more. He can be or do as he desires.

Roy is a frustration to any attempt to clarify or represent what would otherwise be an illusion. He is unseen, unknowable, unfathomable, troubling in description, yet real. Roy is unknowable, yes, but discernable by the fruits of his accomplishments. He fulfills the needs of humans as needs arise. Humans are needy and Roy is needless, yet capable of answering petitions for mercy when not otherwise occupied with great wars that may be in play in DE. Roy is not a thing to be named or described. *Roy* is a term for this *great soul*, as how else could the story be told.

Roy will be revealed, known by a composite of realities. He is best described as three and is as much three as one, and as one as three. Each is a functionary of the *engineer*. Each is equal in essence and attributes, with different purposes. There is the *planner*, the *implementer* and the *reminder*. We have been exposed to all but, for the most part, the *planner*. None is as the mathematically equivalent of a third, but one, no purpose more important than another. Incomprehensible is what you can comprehend. Know the power, strength and glory of Roy from what he has engineered and accomplished thus far. There is more to come.

Roy will be a pneuma that fills humans with his essence; his breath-giving life, filling lungs, and providing energy. Humans will know his presence inside, the believers for sure, finding his counsel and reminders as lanterns illuminating their path to DE. Believers will hear his voice. He has the ability to manifest himself in a recognizable fashion. The extensions of his *being*, all Roy, will serve a purpose as required to exemplify Roy's omni-elements.

Niles is likewise indiscernible. His composition is not the same as Roy. There are similarities, but Niles defiance is not of the essence of Roy.

A contingent of Ontologics was gathered after Niles was defrocked. The smallest, a ball of white dough in appearance, his head protruding from the composite asked the others, "What happened?"

The elder, his marshmallow size greater than the others answered, "His essentials exploded into puzzle pieces that reformed as an altered distorted deformed Ontologic, no longer worthy of inclusion in the council. He is misshaped, given sharpened fangs, and discolored as the shade of embarrassment. If you see him, you will know him. Resist him. Niles can influence humans and impact their lives. He does so in an effort to divert humans from any consideration of the City of Roy and our authority structure and judicial system.

"Niles uses the selfishness of humans to achieve his ends. He focuses on the hypocrite within each person. We must be strong in our efforts to aid *the great soul*. Only Roy is the *supreme judge*. Niles aversion to the commands and directives of Roy, particularly those imparted to the humans in Roy's engineered Terra, made Roy demote Niles, and strip him of his high ranking position in DE. Thus, the altered figure with which he now must contend."

Another Ontologic joined the discussion, "As retribution, Niles took it upon himself to become a force against Roy in DE as well as on Terra. Associates, seraphs, Ontologics which also considered themselves maligned, a fallen class, joined with Niles to gain control. They too were modified in their look. DE is not as tranquil as we would like and humans might assume. Mike is the one assigned to engage Niles as necessary."

Niles position, his station in DE, was replaced with seraphs' Mike and Gabe, associates, attendants, given specific tasks in helping Roy relate, communicate and protect the inhabitants in the domain Terra.

Humans need images. To discuss an object, a person, a thing, Roy, Niles, associates, Ontologics, or seraphs, a conceptual depiction is helpful. In the case of Roy, Niles and others in DE, any picture, drawing or outline is only that of the mind of the person or persons, their own thinking. We need images, even if the images are not in fact those of Roy or any of his associates, even his more controversial, deceptive, or adversarial associates. Humans need to imagine and the mind of man has a vision of Roy. Different minds may have different visions. If viewed the seraphs, the messengers, may be translucent, a dazzling white appearance, clothed in white linen, wearing a belt of gold and jewels, eyes ablaze, hanging above, and yet hidden by the brilliance. Greater perception may be possible for those to whom the seraph will speak or a revelation imparted, providing a clearer image.

An image honors and remembers. Mental pictures can help children and adults better understand a supernatural being never fully captured by human language. Images can evolve in our minds as humans grow, from child to adult the images may become greater, more varied, more reflective of the experiences of life, education, influences and attitudes, and even more commonly accepted.

Roy wants images of him to be freely displayed and love imagined, as an act of worship. As a representation of conscious thought, images provide a connection with Roy and his partners, which were never accurate except that they're reflections of the linkages with Roy, the mind of man experiencing Roy's reality, the reality only that Roy is. If an image of Roy is all-powerful so be it; to destroy such an image would cause pain for the human especially that of a child who thinks nothing bad could ever happen.

Humans have imagined, depicted, and drawn the *beings* of Niles, Mike, Gabe and others from DE.

Images of Niles are generally scary, a being of an arbitrary nature to be feared, in contrast to Roy, who is to be loved. The Niles's image is one of temptation. There are messengers, false prophets advanced by Niles that many on Terra follow. Many Terra-based leaders resist any depiction, preferring not to have any representation in pictures, images, even cartoons. To hide any conceived representation is to possibly hide that which is evil, to not allow the evil nature to be seen, exposed, and made known.

Images of the evil prophet or messenger, the fallen seraph's Terra-choices, would be counterproductive to the goals; those goals in opposition to Roy—wanting the City of Roy defiled. It would make known to humans the visions of dragons, serpents, multiheaded beasts, distended entrails of human failings, and other disfigured, disgusting portraits of a wannabe Roy. The wannabes would be armed to destroy, equipped to fill killing fields with bodies of those considered weak, and also to eliminate persecutors of Niles and his false prophets, seeking any excuse to wage war on Roy's followers.

Roy's image can only be that of love imagined. He so loves Terra he would do anything he could to keep all humans close. His face is what we would all want to see and share, always delightful, always smiling, and always encouraging.

ooooo

Terra and DE are not co-eternal. Terra is finite. The truth of history lies in the book that Roy assembles. Its contents will contain his inspired directives. Events that occurred at the beginning of time and space will be described. It will be informative. Leaders and their roles will be important as examples. The nature of Roy and Niles will be on display. Those who forecast the future will be featured, and their prophecies will come true. False teaching will be condemned. There will be warnings. A life of love, joy, hope, and peace will be featured. Also, a disparaged life apart from Roy will be clarified. The end of Terra will be depicted. Those who embrace the book will have a relationship with Roy and know their future. They will know also that life on Terra will not be easy. DE will continue when Terra ends. The book of the many events of Terra's existence and its inhabitants will be of significant value.

The book Roy places on Terra will be written by believers, by friends of Roy, and breathed out by Roy. It will be the book of the people-of-Roy. It will be Roy quoted as much as Roy remembered. It will be the documented evidence of witnesses recorded, honest as to their recall, and consistent as to the truth. Not all will recall alike, as is the case of witnesses to most Terra events, but they will share the common element of Truth. Roy will cause the hands of the authors to reflect properly on him from various angles, collectively revealing the glory that is Roy. The truth that is his book will be proven.

ooooo

Wars exist in DE. The battles of DE are ongoing, light vs. darkness, the good vs. the evil, and can occupy Roy or the associates' focus, taking them from immediately responding to the calls of those who believe in Roy on Terra. The *believers'* petitions are heard, but it may take a few measured periods of time for the response to arrive. Mike and Gabe are DE generals, associates, Ontologics, in Roy's battalion of security, protection, and defense. There are forces that require Roy's attention and the work of the associates. The same associates often are assigned to protect classes of humans and individuals on Terra. The opposing sides of the battlefield in DE represent *light* and *darkness*. Roy is *light* and the all powerful force that heads DE, but he's not without detractors.

Those fallen from the grace of Roy and upset with his policies or position or accomplishments go to the dark corner. Their jealous nature then goes on display—their actions portraying their desires and selfish goals. The associates having a similar fate go with the others. Niles and his accomplices grow in number. Skirmishes in DE occur. Protests and outright fisticuffs ensue, each conflict an attempt to dethrone Roy, in part or in entirety. Only in DE can the one that is Roy be seen by associates and challenged.

Nothing we can comprehend can fathom this other-Terra fight as we can only consider the lesser battles on Terra. That is what we know, while at the same time there are much greater barriers being defended; we will never understand the extreme cage fighting—where pits of tension, hatred, venom, and rage were being unleashed in DE. It is expected that the worst of all trials, periods of suffering, much trouble will ensue in DE as the gathering of forces of Niles attempts to exterminate every descendant of the leaders of Roy.

There will be an unprecedented time of distress for Terra. Niles will be the reason and cause of such distress. Roy will, let it be known, protect and save, in the form of a national deliverance for all who favor Roy; it will not be as a class, as a liberation contingent, but as individuals who repent, accept, and give thanks. Those, who lose their lives for Roy, will have a new life, even a new body. From a sleep, they will arise to take their place in the everlasting DE, assuming positions of honor. They will shine as bright as the seraphs.

The forms, the seraphs, in DE are alive, awake, and whole. They are of one mind, different, joined, and shared. The mind of humans is found and united with Roy and his associates (good and bad). Humans are closest to the unimaginable Roy, yet not the same. Roy and his associates can appear, and do appear, in ways made recognizable to man, more to avoid the fear of their actual appearance. If, and who knows, they were to be as they are, humans could not possibly accept them as a saving force; the fear would be far too great. Roy has man imagine Roy as Roy wishes. Man can only see what the truth is. Such truth when found is divinely revealed. Man, knowing the truth, is fully capable as a means of preserving the *self.* When focused on the *me,* in whatever is heard or read, denying *truth,* man in turn is denying the reality of Roy.

This has been said and is worth repeating—the accomplishments in the formation of the cosmos, the support systems, Terra, and humans, were caused by Roy's applied intellect—an intellect above all intellects. Describing the mind of Roy is simply not possible. Humans were given minds, intelligence, and still find it impossible, even among the most intelligent of humanity, to consider this intelligible source of all that comprises Terra. For the brightest of the humans, the mind of Roy remains unfathomable. No other living system, animal, or material elements, comes close to the mind of man. The mind of humans is as close to Roy as humans will ever come; it is what distinguishes humans from everything else on Terra. If you were able to measure the intellectual spread between animals and humans that mathematical figure could be multiplied by infinity to picture the spread between humans and Roy.

Niles is aware also that mind control is a means to achieve his ends. He sees man as vulnerable.

The *intelligence* of Terra is inherent in the animal kingdom. How they co-exist is a function of the role they play. On display and in action evil acts committed by the animal kingdom reflect flaws or willful wants. There are, however, attributes of Terra that only require the intelligence of Roy having no independent thought. That which is without intellect is without evil as nothing can tempt that which is mindless. We see the beauty of the mountains, streams, valleys, trees, plants, and oceans. Such beauty can only be altered at the hand or direction of Roy, yet they remain beautiful. Even in the destructive forces of nature there is beauty; the awe caused by the power of the relational elements of space, the cosmos, operating to maintain balance is unexpected, unpredictable, and at times terrifying. Humans have freedom by choice and thus can choose an alternative to Roy. Roy would label such an alternative as evil, and allow, as Niles has been allowed, the existence of evil. Yet, from the outset, the plan is for evil to be destroyed. It is a test for humans to pass or fail.

The human mind becomes weak in the presence of a seraph of Roy or Roy himself—legs quiver and to their knees men fall. There is fear of the supernatural. Unknown yet a presence felt, trembling, shaky, and fainting spells occur. Eyes will be hidden; those chosen will fall to the ground, afraid. Strength will return when the supernatural force by touching restores the heart and strength of the recipient. Assured and composed humans can know the associates of Roy, and Roy himself, are caring, loving, and encouraging by nature. Revelations, prophetic insight may be provided and understood.

"Do not be afraid," expressed in calm, soothing, confident tones are heard by those that doubt, feel a presence, and need reassurance.

Man's love of Roy requires a level of devotion that makes suffering unavoidable. Roy needed humans to believe in him and accept his calling, standing firm also in his defense against the tactics of Niles. Believing humans must deal with their personal stain, large or small, to demonstrate love and obedience to the maker of the cosmos.

Niles appeal is easier to accept, yet provides empty promises than cannot be sustained or continuously fulfilling.

Roy's promise of a life eternal in DE, with him, takes courage to accept and an application of all principles of proper living on Terra. Even all the proper living, though, cannot overcome the selfish nature of man exposed by *the lie*. Humans were to be as living sacrificed to the realm of Roy, suffering for the glory of DE, losing their lives for *Roy* as necessary to maintain awareness that Roy was their *engineer*.

We are all part of Roy's plan and none other.

Roy Visits Terra

Roy made a most significant personal visit. He prepared for this coming to Terra carefully.

From his vantage point overlooking Terra, Roy asked Gabe to see him. He arrived to join Roy observing the moving puzzle and events transpiring. Roy spoke, "Events are taking place on Terra where obedience to me has been compromised. No one can satisfy the standards that we have provided and even they have produced. It is a mess. What I desire as order is now chaotic. We correct one group, but it does not take long and they continue to deny their hearts and succumb to other influences, none of which are fulfilling.

"They say they are people of Roy, but do not act accordingly. They follow Niles, err in judgment, then make sacrifices, and seek forgiveness. It is a never ending cycle. It is hopeless. We need to provide universal forgiveness. We need to make them aware life in not meaningless; it is, however, without me in it. We need to restore hope and joy."

"It is broken. I think I understand," was Gabe's response.

"I am going to Terra," Roy said.

"But how? No one would know you, and they cannot see you."

"I will transform myself into a nature similar to man. I will remain, who I am, eternal. At the same time to be accepted, I will appear as a marvelous perfect human, two-in-one as it were. I will look every bit a human. I will be as the ambassador of Dimension Eternal. I expected this and my visit has been predicted."

Roy knew what was possible. Roy knew what was necessary; after all, he did make man.

Seeing himself as the *engineer*, as the author of Terra and its history, it was possible for Roy to place himself as a character in his story. He would declare his presence as two natures, that of Roy and that of his Terra-present nature.

Roy continued, "I will be of the race of the people-of-Roy. Living among them, I will be able to demonstrate, guide, and teach the ways of living as required. I will be the example to everyone. To those with whom I shared, what I revealed to them as a caveat of what's to happen is about to transpire."

But he would be so much more. This functionary of Roy would save those that believe when Terra ends.

"Freedom of choice has tested and corrupted man and made it impossible for the greatest or the least of humans to ever gain access to DE. The freedoms will not be removed. They test who can be my friend. Not everyone can be saved, but I will enable those that believe in my incarnation to enjoy access to this glorious eternal place."

Roy was enthusiastic and confident.

"Why not eliminate all freedom? Eliminate those that disobey?" Gabe asked.

"That would not allow for acts of grace, nor distinguish on Terra a tolerant and loving people. Those that demonstrate their love, as I love, will more likely be my followers. They must love their neighbors, even those that are not followers, as they love me.

"Resistance to temptations provides the means for individuals to prove to themselves they are worthy. Loving me, the one they only sense made Terra and all that exists, takes courage and faith. I have provided evidence in everything they see or feel. Yet, it is easy to stray and find acceptance of the known, elements of humans, addictive human made substances and offerings easy to attach to; thus, they deny the supernatural."

"I have a job for you in all of this," Roy said.

Gabe asked, "What is that?"

"Gabe, you need to keep everyone at ease. Those closest to my birth on Terra must be made aware of their special status. Inform those humans I use. Tell them what is about to happen. Do what is needed to enable this advent of my transformation into a life-form on Terra."

"Yes, my *great soul*. I will do as you request. I am honored," Gabe responded humbly.

"It will still be me, Gabe, but in the form designed to live on Terra," Roy said.

"I understand. You can do as you wish. Nothing is too difficult for you."

"I will be born on Terra," Roy announced.

"What?" Gabe said as he swallowed.

"Born on Terra", Roy continued.

"You heard me. It has already been forecast, as you know. It will not be the same as a human birth. I will be born of a virgin."

"Why a virgin? Although, I think I know," came Gabe's reply.

"For purity. My birth on Terra will be without the polluted strain of DNA that flows through humans. As pure as A-man was, his strain was polluted by disobedience. My essence in the womb will cleanse the DNA of the virgin mom making possible a perfect human, a new A-man, without the stain of Niles's *lie*. It is the only way this can happen. I will be pure, without any imperfections. The soul of this human will be mine. And I will not succumb to the temptations of Niles. It must be that way. It is part of my plan," Roy explained.

"So be it. As you wish." Gabe accepted the plan.

"There will be a new deal, a new agreement with the humans. To this point it has been difficult to understand they can have a relationship with me. Now they will know it is possible. There will be doubters, and those who will always deny me, but certainly the evidence of my presence on Terra will be useful and meaningful to those whose hearts are open and properly focused," said Roy.

ooooo

It all went quite smoothly. Carefully selected, a woman, Miriam, was made pregnant, informed then by Gabe, certainly to her surprise.

She was seated outside her adobe cottage. She felt a tug on her right shoulder. She turned. There was nothing. She heard a voice, "Fear not, I will not harm you."

"What?" She reacted, stood, turned around, but saw nothing. She sat down. Looking forward, she then saw before her a shadow, a form similar to a stack of hay, but opaque.

Then she heard a voice.

"I have been sent to tell you how special you are. You have been chosen by Roy to be the mother to his essence on earth."

Another, "What" was emitted from her mouth. She bent forward.

"You will be the mother of Roy's child, a divine human."

"I am not married. How?" came the response from Miriam.

"Roy can do and be as he wishes. You will be cared for. You have been impregnated with his pneuma to give birth to Roy on Terra. He will be called Rom."

She rose. Her hands covered one another on her belly, Miriam said, "I am pregnant?"

"Yes. You have Roy with you," Gabe said to her.

Miriam was from the linage of the people-of-Roy. So was her husband to be. This act would enable Roy to show man how *self* is impeding the right path. Through his essence on Terra he would unveil *self* in such a way that mankind would know the end journey—man stripped of ego, pure and devoted. All souls are repositories for Roy's pneuma, each individual however receives his fill depending on their relationship with Roy. The pneuma in remission by the circumstances surrounding *the lie* could be brought to life anew.

Miriam was chosen. She readily realized she was now blessed with an awesome task, but one with consequences, embarrassment and suffering along the way.

Her fiancé stood up for her and accepted her condition. He was a man of faith. He married her, and they prepared for the delivery.

ooooo

The day came. Miriam had a loving companion and now husband, Jordan. She suffered evil glances during her pregnancy by those seeing her as a sinful woman. But she gave birth to a beautiful baby boy. It was a great day. As she sat with her newborn in her arms, swaddled, unexpected visitors arrived.

"How did you know we were here? And why are you here?" she asked. Jordan stood prepared to offer a defense if necessary.

"We were told by Roy. He informed us and provided a guiding light to follow. It led us here. We want to be in the presence of this boy who will one day become a savior to all people. We brought gifts that will help you to raise your child and to protect him until the time is right."

"When will that be?" asked Jordan.

"Only the boy will know." This was the collective response from three of those in attendance.

ooooo

Miriam, Jordan, and the baby lived quietly for years as the baby boy grew. He was named Ram.

A part of Roy since the *beginning*, Roy-the-man, Roy-as-man, in human form, was new to Terra. A person as Terra never experienced—perfect in every way, yet poor, humble, and respectful of others. He aided in the initiation and engineering of Terra. He knew Terra. He was in Roy, of Roy, and as Roy.

Now transformed, he could always answer the question, "Who are you?" with the simple answer, "I am the I Am."

It may be confusing. He was saying he was Roy. That truth would present itself as *master*, the perfect *master* for all to follow. He would accompany mankind, teach them, and clarify the transformation needed to properly reach Roy's DE.

For a few decades Roy roamed Terra as Roy-the-man, as an offspring of Roy, Ram, leading a life consistent with established standards. From birth to puberty to manhood he grew. He relied on others when away from home to provide shelter and food. Only in his last few years was his appearance felt to such an extent that even today all of Terra remembers. Roy knew man—their criminal nature, the humans he formed, but he wanted them to understand Roy better. Ram had a handpicked cadre of close followers. They were his companions as he traversed the land of his people. They would be the witnesses to miracles and Ram's crusade. Labeled the Intuits they would come to know the ultimate reality—Ram and Roy had an inseparable union. They were *one*.

A cousin preceded Ram and was known as JB. His parents were elderly, having been blessed with a child in their later years after much praying. JB left home in his early teens to live with a group of devotees—all men—that revered Roy; they were dedicated, and taught a right way of life. They were knowledgeable of the words that had been printed about Roy, a history already reported. As a group, they patiently waited for the arrival of the *savior*, a savior already predicted.

The arrival was foretold by persons who spoke and wrote of the future with the authority and blessing of Roy. The group had been filled temporarily with the functionary pneuma of Roy and imparted with a certain wisdom. JB was filled too with the pneuma and Roy's expectations. When separated from the isolated seaside compound of his new family, JB would walk the *land* and lecture, proclaiming the desires of Roy to any who would listen. He also spoke of the coming of one much greater than himself.

At one occasion while JB was speaking to a crowd, he saw Ram. He went to him. They embraced. JB then announced to everyone, "This is the one who is greatest of all in the eyes of Roy. Know him, and know he will one day provide freedom as no other can possibly do."

A glow, an aura, illuminated the head of Ram. JB placed his hands on Ram's shoulders, facing him. Those around were in awe. Ram raised his arms, hands above his head, and nodded to the people. Facing JB, he said, "Thank you."

Then he moved through those assembled and went on his way.

Ram walked about traversing every corner of his small homeland. He visited with many, touched the lives of many, and performing many wonders of his own. He came to be known as a person possessing unique qualities. He was a healer. He was an advisor. He was kind, caring and loving to all with whom he came in contact with. He was tested by Niles but never gave in; he was perfect and sinless. Ram developed a significant following.

ooooo

During that time, Roy made a decision. Humans continue to this day to have difficulty fully realizing, fully appreciating, and fully knowing what was meant. Roy caused the greatest suffering that would ever be to happen; he did this for all humans. This, again, was done for a reason.

He called for Gabe. When he arrived Roy was pacing.

"Gabe, do you understand what I am about to do—what I need to do?"

"I am uncertain," said Gabe.

So the reply went, "Roy, you know what is best, and your plan is the plan for Terra, past, present, and future. I am here to serve you."

"Man needs to be punished for accepting *the lie*, and the constant temptations offered up by Niles. Humans cannot substitute themselves for me. They need to rid themselves of self and accept the provisions I make readily available. They have been filled with doubts, flawed, by Niles' enticements. Yet I remain everywhere available to provide. They are disobedient people, particularly where the GND is concerned. I know they can never be perfect.

Never. No one will be right with me unless I do what I have to do. Am I making myself clear?"

Gabe could only answer, "Yes" but not without some concern.

He said, "Roy, to date, humans could sacrifice a perfect animal to atone for sins."

Roy's response, "Yes, but…but they continue to make mistakes, and will continue to make mistakes. The sacrifices made were insufficient; a device of man. It only made man aware of the crimes they committed for which they needed to seek my forgiveness. They need to know that believing in me, and living according to one's belief, has rewards. It is believing that matters. No one can earn their way into my court. They must believe in me. I can and will free humans from their flawed nature. Through this act of extreme punishment I will do for humans more than they can do for themselves. It will make a future with me possible."

Roy went on to say, "What I am about to do will alter Terra. It will save mankind."

His mouth agape Gabe spoke, "I will do whatever. I know I cannot appear in a way other than what humans will understand. Just let me know how I can assist. I will have others available to work with me to insure your success."

The people-of-Roy were continuously disrespectful of the laws, the GND, the Tablet Laws, and could never be perfect. Crimes committed by man in deference to Roy's outline were crimes against Roy, no matter the magnitude. At the time any crime against Roy would result in condemnation to a most unpleasant eternal future. Just one evil was enough; there was no offset possible by doing what was right. Roy was not to be disregarded. It was for DE, Roy wanted to correct the errors of man, not for Terra, but the proper condition of man would enable the founders of a great nation to frame a constitution as none other.

Roy attempted to convince man they were failures, to know the truth of their hopelessness, of their need to try harder, and to be more disciplined and obey. Daily reminders were needed. He often subjected them to his vengeance and wrath. Examples of the outcome for the mistakes made were insufficient to provide restitution from what is the innate nature of man. Humans know what is right, yet they are imperfect, made so by the freedom of choice and the fruit of the forbidden tree.

The perfected human form had hidden imperfections. Early in the garden, they first made a choice, at the first opportunity, to be selfish. Roy condemned humans forever, and Roy's justice required eternal separation. That justice needed alteration and only Roy could accomplish that. All natures of punishment were devised for crimes committed, large and small. Man's error was simply the impossibility of meeting the rules, regulations, and laws put forward by Roy as transcribed by man, chosen *leaders* at that.

The GND did not work for them. It was the perfect storm of never being able to be perfect. The condemnation was to no avail. Man continued to miss the mark. They atoned for mistakes by killing perfect animals, but then needed to do so again, and again. The methods of atonement were to no avail. Roy's established target was a total obedience to the program. Humans had an imperfect aim, defiance toward Roy's laws. What was Roy to do? Roy continued to explain to Gabe the reason for his action.

"Gabe, this is my objective. Humans need a change of heart, a heart for what has been made possible for them, a true connection. Man's physical form has been infected with original sin, the freedom of will, causing leanings toward Niles. This will not end until Niles is destroyed. We will allow the gates of DE to open to them. Justification for a committed and dutiful focus on me needs a sacrifice as none other.

"Ram is the example needed so man can see the truth. I will suffer for mankind by taking and accepting the severest chastisement only they deserve. Each individual will be provided the tool of saving grace. It will not be a collective community liberated from sin. Although all mankind would be included, each person will need a receptive heart. Thus, not everyone will be saved."

The laws reflected the obstacle man must overcome. The GND became a multiple of hurdles over which man ran a race without end. The hurdles were either too high, too wide, or too deep.

"Gabe, this new promise will enable man to escape his physical dimension and enter the spiritual dimension. No man can complete that race without this sacrifice. Man's selfish diversion away from the divine is the reality of the impossibility of perfection."

Roy was to construct a new highway, to pave the way recognizing the sins of free will and Niles temptations as the driver of the corrupted flesh. There would be suffering, repentance, perseverance, and trials of all kinds. Roy's laws would be heeded, as humanly possible; there would be a striving for Roy with the objective to make Roy's kingdom accessible. Roy was about to provide the handicapped, all mankind, a ramp to his many rooms. To have eternal life was to have new meaning and new understanding. Man required a relationship with Roy. Knowing Roy was the ultimate goal. Apart from Roy, life on Terra would have no meaning and no purpose.

Roy took it upon himself to provide the ultimate sacrifice, take the hit, for all man had done, does, and would do—all evils large and small. Sensing the imperfections, a means was devised to overcome them and allow a pathway to DE. It was the start of The Great Transfer.

His functionary on Terra, Ram, would be used, a perfect human without corrupted DNA. His essence was Roy. Roy would allow his offspring to be put to death by human standards as punishment for human crimes more perceived than actual. At that time all the crimes of man past, present, and future that would be or will be committed against Roy would be included in the proclamation of punishment on Ram, man's burdens to be Ram's burdens, the iniquities of everyone to be included in Ram's sentence to death. This perfect specimen would suffer for mankind. It was Roy's predetermined method to atone for all mankind's mistakes. It was *grace*.

ooooo

A conversation took place.

Approaching the moment of Roy's final act, Ram spoke to, talking directly to Roy. As if speaking out loud to himself, Ram, the human element, would converse with Roy, the divine element. It was a verbal exchange with the inevitable.

Ram was first to speak, "As much as I have accomplished on Terra, there's more to do."

Roy said, "Yes, my son, I know. But it is time. What you have accomplished will be remembered, and what you are about to do will never be forgotten. It will be contested, it will be denied, and it will be transformative, but never forgotten."

"I am not ready! There is more that I can do," more a plea by Ram for more time than a request to not go forward.

With his eyes lifted, his eyebrows raised, Ram said, "Even though I am not ready, I will do as you desire. I am prepared. I have prepared the Intuits, yet they do not fully comprehend. They will though."

"Mankind is needy, and needs you now. Our love for all humans will prevail." Roy responded.

"Do not forsake me," were the next words from Ram's mouth.

At that moment, Ram was burdened with the weight of every sin. Piled high with the excrement from human's disregard for Roy, on display he was disgraced, punished, and destroyed.

Roy continued, "Your humanity is to be no more; your divinity is to provide the saving pathway to DE. You will return in unity with me. You will be all of mankind-as-one in overcoming the barrier which can now never enable humans to enter DE. You are man's replacement in this ultimate saving act. Justice will be restored. We have a need for new *associates*, which cannot be satisfied in the present condition of man.

"Even those that have lived in the past that may be acceptable will not be without this next step. You have made it known that which is the *truth*; you are the solution; you are the means.

You provided the example. Only you! There will be future false attempts to represent our glory, but only this act of graciousness will be needed. Nothing will compare to this act of *mercy*."

"Oh my, I know you are correct. This is like talking to myself," said Ram with a bit of levity. To all observers, his pain was extreme.

Roy again said, "You are talking to yourself, and me. One more thing, what you have achieved, the example you have already provided, will be as a light shining on the path to DE. I know you feel you have more to do. You must know the Intuits, and those, who believe, know you and have faith, will continue to make known the truth. Through them our presence on Terra will always be. As man's substitute, you will make right with me those that understand, have faith, and their spiritual separation from DE and me will end."

Ram acknowledged, "I know."

Roy continued, "If you have not considered second chances, now you should. You will live on, as I live on, in me, and in man. We are *one*. Together we will sit to the left, you to right, of the command post and division lectern to welcome and embrace those who have obeyed and loved as we have. Now humans will be able to be reborn in the pneuma of our unconditional love. It will be our assurance, the pneuma within, that the punishment you are about to suffer and the sacrifice you are about to make opens the gates to DE for those that follow.

"You will depart, be entombed, and will be restored to appear to many, including the Intuits. Your grave will be bare. This resurrection will be all the proof necessary of the truth of what we have said, inspired, and recorded. All will know you and I are one. It will make obvious my truth is the same always. It is objective truth just as gravity and the sun rising in the east.

"There will be a new program in Terra. All will be forgiven who believe in what you will have done. They remain wired with the potential to make errors in judgment, but will repent and atone when they do err, knowing their faith has made them free. You have fulfilled the laws and they are always forgiven. We will know their hearts. If their hearts be true, they will be applauded when they arrive in DE. Justification will only be by their faith in you. The test will be the extent they pursue a relationship with us.

"A-man is about to be given a second chance, an opportunity to restore a life eternal destroyed by *the lie of Niles*."

ooooo

Roy used Terra-based self-appointed ministers of the Tablet Laws and even more laws, those added by man, to condemn Ram. These ministers judged humans according to the strictest standards of the law based upon their interpretation. If tested even they could not meet the standards. At the same time these ministers failed to fully know Roy, always seeking the *me* in words spoken when deciding how they themselves would be impacted. They were not loving or caring as much as callous and overbearing. They most wanted to protect their authority and power base.

Ram, having exposed their personal contempt for Roy before the people, became a threat. They made note of Ram's influence. He was unworthy in their view. The people were beginning to respect Ram more than the local authorities. He needed to be eliminated.

They focused on Ram's proclamation that he was one with his father, implying his father was Roy. It was blasphemous to them and cause for condemnation. They would destroy this fake. In death, the truth that was said to be would no longer exist. The threat eliminated; their authority enhanced. So they thought.

When the opportunity arose a local platoon from the army was assigned to take Ram into custody. A man, once a friend of Ram, was with the platoon as it approached. The commander asked him, "Which one is Ram?"

The betrayer pointed and said, "He is the one." His finger extended. It was as if kissed by Niles himself. The soldiers knew he was the one the authorities wanted removed.

This all was in compliance with Roy's Plan.

ooooo

Ram carried the burdens of man on his shoulders, punished with each step he took to his final place of death, and his last breath. Ram knew that Roy who sent him was always with him. Ram would always do what was pleasing to Roy, never tempted, and an example to all mankind. Unblemished he offered himself to Roy. While humans were still sinners Ram died for them. They were saved from the wrath of Roy. In their fleshlike existence the temptations of Niles remained.

Ram came to seek and save the lost. For the sake of all mankind Roy made Ram the criminal, who was no criminal, so that men would be correct with, even pleasing to, Roy. What man then did would be a by-product of knowing Roy. Those that believed and were thankful, knowing, and understanding this incomprehensible act of sacrifice, would do *good works* out of respect, love, and devotion to Ram. It was not a merit system, but a willful desire to live by the example Ram provided. Man's eyes were opened, their hearts laid bare to the true nature of Roy. Many would accept and be most thankful.

This was The Great Transfer.

Ram became the substitute for man, placing on himself all mankind's errors. Everyone of them, as if he was each and every man. What he had already done for man would continue when all else was over, and when the curtain on the stage of life on Terra would fall. His spilled blood was the cleanser that would restore the defiled container that the human had become. Their disobedience to *the lie* would be forgiven. From the time of *the lie* to The Great Transfer man had no way of gaining Roy's favor and acceptance into DE. By his act and proof of life after death mankind would know that Ram was the reality and the truth. Humans would know the love Roy had for them, having made a world for them, only them, containing everything they would require. Man too would be free to make the future their opportunity and not be constrained by the past or their criminal nature.

ooooo

The Intuits would be used by Roy to spread the message of Ram to the corners of Terra. They would overcome their fears and their selfishness. The truth of Ram became their reality. His return to life erased their doubts. They lived the rest of their lives for the honor and glory of Ram. They were filled with the Pneuma of Roy.

Roy would never give up on man.

This was a period of emphasis and revelation in mankind's education.

Ram became the center pole of the cosmos around which all would spin. He provided the eyes through which Roy would guide and enrich Terra, expressing his total love and regard for what he accomplished. The quest for man would be made most clear—the love, the mystery would be revealed. Detached and bewildered, man would come to sense the unifying influence of Roy's descendant and become more a part of Roy than ever before. Man would see himself as in a mirror and know his end game.

The Intuits were called upon to go forth and make disciples of all. More disciples would follow in their footsteps all proclaiming Ram has saved mankind. They would inform also of the simplicity of the steps needed to be taken to benefit from Ram's saving sacrifice. Wherever they travel they would tell the people, "Just believe in Ram."

ooooo

Roy's love would abound. Civil laws would become the means for punishment, while Roy retained the final say on Judgment Day. Not Terra-judgment, but judgment in DE. Proper justice was restored as all men would not be condemned. There were many that would be saved.

The established standards provided by Roy and his *leaders* would be guidelines for life on Terra, but more so useful as evidence on Judgment Day. Those that accepted Roy, Ram, and through their actions on Terra reveal true faith would have life eternal with Roy.

Civil authorities could decide on the more meaningful and the lesser crimes and establish their own platform for control, punishment, and harmony among humans. Separating civil law from Roy's GND, man's authority and Roy's would be enabled. Man was not to act for Roy. Roy would always remain the final *punisher*—his sovereignty would be known. Ram, as a functionary of Roy, would be the *advocate* for the faithful. The *pneuma* would be the *guarantor*. Roy, however, beseeched man and the civil leaders to obey applying common sense to the most critical of the moral and ethical values put forward historically. Roy chose those that would lead, and did so for a reason, whether good leaders or bad.

ooooo

Niles, unfortunately, would be ever present, his conflict with Roy ongoing. Roy, knowing this, encouraged man to change, alter his ways, and follow Roy, his descendant, as an act of free will. He warned humans continuously of the endgame, the events that would transpire when Roy's gavel would finally fall. The humans for Roy would be safe; those against Roy condemned.

ooooo

In summary—from DE, Roy visited Terra, became a human (Ram) and lived a perfect existence. Ram was Roy's own example of excellence; he demonstrated perfection; he aided others, healed others, even awoke persons from the dead; he upset the authorities in the area diminishing their influence; he was condemned to death; he was burdened with the crimes of man and sentenced to die; as a human he died a horrific death to the surprise and at the time disappointment of those who came to be with him personally.

Miriam was a witness.

He was buried.

After only a few days at a place where the Intuits were gathered they noted the presence of another? "Could it be?"

It was Ram, he was alive, or was he? Was that possible?

He spoke, "Do not fear. I have died, but I have overcome the death human's experience to return to you as proof of my divine nature. As proof also of the truth that I have spoken. Now you will know that all I have shared with you and told you is fact. It is the truth."

The Intuits stared at Ram and after a few moments began to relax. Following a meal together Ram was suddenly gone.

Ram had appeared after death, as no human could ever do, transgressed, witnessed by hundreds of humans including those he befriended while on his Terra, the Intuits at first. He overcame physical death to live spiritually. The Great Transfer was complete. His form of death exceeded in pain anything humans might conceptualize. The duration of the suffering endured was extreme torture. The Intuits could do nothing to help him; they were afraid. His outcome was predestined. He became the center of focus for life itself, a mystery revealed, the goal and purpose of man made more evident.

ooooo

What happened? Roy allowed for the guards overseeing the demise of Ram to entomb him. The guards first insured Ram was dead. Then they wrapped his maimed limp body in linens, placed him on a stretcher and carried him to the tomb. He was laid inside and the tomb entrance covered by a massive heavy wheel made of rock. Two guards were left at the tomb for the night. Why, the question could be asked, were guards needed to protect this cadaver. Were the authorities concerned something would happen, the body stolen, or something even totally unexpected? In the morning women came to anoint the body with perfume. The guards rose to push the rock aside to expose the tomb only to discover it partially moved already. Surprised, yet they proceeded. Everyone then stopped and gasped.

"It is empty!" They exclaimed in unison.

There was no body inside. The gauze linen cloth was neatly folded on the stone slab on which Ram's deceased body had been placed.

"Where is he?" the women asked.

"Have you been here all night?"

The guards stood tall, "Yes, and we have no idea."

"How can this possibly be? Where is our beloved Ram?" the woman cried out.

At that instant there was a loud clap of thunder. The group jumped—startled. The women sensed a presence and were called from that place.

The day prior at the hour of Ram's death there was also thunder. Terra shook. Curtains were torn.

About twenty or thirty feet from the burial site a man caught up with the women. He was recognized. It was Ram. One of them fell to her knees, shaking and trembling. The others stood, their hands crossed, covered their mouths. Ram placed his hand, still showing signs of torture, on her shoulder, "Do not be afraid."

At that she rose, "Are you...."

"Yes, I am as you suspect. I did die. Now I am with Roy, and you are to inform the Intuits of this." With that said, Ram departed.

Ram arose from the dead, Gabe assisting, no longer human, existing in an interstitial locale at times as Ram, and as an apparition able to pass through natural things in ways no one had ever done—thus at times a supernatural *wonder* (Roy). By Ram rising up, overcoming death, it was proof that all the crimes of man were overcome. Had just one remained Ram would have failed, his spiritual rising-up would not have occurred. Death has no power where there is no sin. This extended beyond the limits of ordinary experience. He was present in his ultimate nature, supremely good, transcendent and immanent. He instilled a renewed excitement and made the truth he shared indeed Truth.

The Intuits heard from the women of this wonder. No one ever before rose from the dead. They gathered to discuss this phenomenon. Ram unexpectedly entered the room. He calmed them. They asked what was taking place.

"I will be with you for a month or so and then no longer as you now see me," Ram informed them.

He then went on to say, "This is to provide emphasis to what I have shared with you. But I will remain with you, as Roy, as Ram, as my *pneuma* living in you, reminding you as a counselor, providing comfort, and ensuring you of your place in our eternal realm. DE will welcome all who believe in me."

The Intuits were witnesses. Man was to know, even those not present, this sacrifice was the truth of their salvation. Grace came to all who accepted Ram.

The concept of one man *risen* had never before been considered. Even though this time period after his death, his interstitial existence, lasted only for a month and one-half, it became like an era, a transforming time never to be forgotten by humans. It was and is the greatest *wonder* of Terra

ooooo

Roy so loved Terra he gave Ram, so humans would have access to DE. They would know the valleys they must cross and the bridges they must use to reach the gates at the entry to DE. Travel would not be easy, the major impediment being man himself. A guide was provided. Instilled with Roy's *pneuma*, the Intuits aided as ongoing guides, docents, to the kingdom of DE. Roy's pneuma was to be made alive in those who understood the reality of Ram's generous act of sacrifice.

The pneuma that went into remission at the time of A-man's disobedient act was to be re-ignited in those who voluntarily accepted Ram's plight and were thankful.

In one series of actions Ram succeeded in freeing humans from being bound by a strict adherence to the established legal-

istic system which endured for thousands of years. Laws established by Roy and promoted by humans consumed people-of-
Roy. Others were simply lawless, self-directed, and making it up
as they go. They were correct laws in every fashion, but Roy now
knew it was not humanly possible for man to be right with the
laws. All mankind was to be included in his new covenant.

It is as if the proclamation was made stating, "The result of
one error of judgment made by A-man was condemnation for
all men. So, the result of one act of righteousness by Ram was
justification that brings life for all men making many righteous
and able to qualify for a life-eternal in DE. It is and will be a
new beginning for all men and women. It is the end of the law,
so there may be righteousness for everyone who believes. It is by
grace, not by having the weight of right actions exceeding wrong
actions, that man is now saved for DE."

ooooo

It was as two dimensions—the first, DE, a dwelling for the divine,
and the second was Terra. Between the two is a chasm. The corrupted DNA possessed humans lived in Terra and could only
peer at the other side, all too often covered in clouds, hard to see
or imagine. DE contains Roy, functionaries, and the Ontologics.
They could oversee Terra, but failed in many ways to instill in
the humans the life-ethic needed to cross over the chasm. At the
same time, Niles and other outcast-ontologics battled Roy and
his team for the souls of humans.

Ram's birth, perfect life, and example—his sacrificial death
was as a bridge, a means by which humans can readily cross over
the chasm from Terra to DE, as followers of Ram, and thus as
followers of Roy. Roy, by bringing himself to life on Terra and in
the functionary form of Ram, enacted judgment and justice on
the Niles corrupted humans. He provided a pathway, an escape,
and an opportunity to be eternally thankful.

The history of mankind was laid out in its most explicit form—from death of the pneuma to birth of the pneuma, a restoring of those who comprehend all truth and realize the need for a *savior*. It was a matter of recognizing one is unable to serve Roy and be a slave to *the lie* at the same time. That is the *good news*. You already know the *bad news*.

ooooo

Ram showed Niles (and Niles's adherents) that his death was not the end but a beginning to a new era which would enable considerable progress. Roy embraced all of humanity regardless of status, sex, religion, or those with or without the tattoo. The visible, physical tattoo was no longer needed or recognized. It became a *Terra for all*. The tattoo of those who believed in Ram was internal; it was the pneuma.

Roy became the object for *all*. If the object became their devotion, then obedience to the legalistic framework exemplified historically would be met as a matter of desire, voluntarily, and not as an obligation. Humans were not to control their kind using Roy as their excuse; they were to change their hearts, to have a heart for Roy, his descendant, and his kingdom, willingly, with desire, stripped of ego, content knowing they would one day be in DE. Freedom would reign and Ram coupled with Roy would be seen as the combined supernatural force that it was and is.

Ram returned to DE to be one with Roy. The *pneuma* remained to be with the believers.

ooooo

The *old story* at this juncture was Niles's winning the battle for the souls and hearts of humans. The *old story* provided demonstrations of Roy's ill-temper, his justice, and his vengeance. Humans, however, found other outlets for their desires. The only justice in the *old* was condemnation for all. The *new story*, even though

Niles remained pitted against Roy, showed Niles, who had the upper hand, overcome by love. The humans of Terra had been shown the way to the DE, the bridge they can cross, and now had to only accept the love of Roy and follow. It remained a choice, but one with assurances of the reward of a life eternal, spiritually revived, with Roy.

ooooo

The close followers of Ram, the Intuits, became *leaders* as well as compilers of his presence on Terra. As agents for Roy, they made known his accomplishments and his talk. He had instructed them that post his interstitial phase another *counselor* would remain with them forever. The presence of Ram, and Roy himself would remain in the hearts, minds, and souls of his human followers and leaders. The *counselor* would be present as both teacher and a reminder of everything Ram would have said to them; the *counselor* was Roy's *pneuma*. This counselor would know Ram was divine.

Like ice, water, and vapor, Roy was here in all three thermodynamic stages in which he could be—a composite unity of Roy—*Roy*. As ice, he was the rock, foundational. As water, he was the living essence of Roy. As steam (vapor), he was the pneuma—three as one, all the same H_2O. Whether the ocean, the sea, a stream, a river, a rill, a pond, a lake, a droplet, a snowflake, a bubble or a brook, they are all water; they flow as one, as *Roy*, a universal grantor of life.

Roy saw the need for a bridge between the human groups; a bridge to cross an abyss of hostility dividing one kind from another. By way of the ultimate sacrifice, he destroyed the gap between, filled the chasm, and in his mysterious fashion brought mankind together under one promise. With his blessing, his love, providing mercy to all—as he may have before provided his oldest followers—followers he had initially chosen in the hope they would be his leaders. His sacrifice would save Terra.

Roy's *promise* was very important. The *promise* was given many years past to the son of Roy's first *leader-friend*. At the same time Roy, at the request of the *leader-friend*, only gave a *blessing* to the *leader's* boy born out of wedlock, the son of the *leader* and his wife's maidservant. It was now, however, a *promise* for *all*, available to all mankind, with one condition. The beneficiaries of the *promise* would need to understand and have faith in *Roy* (the composite *Roy*—consisting of Roy, Ram, and Roy's pneuma). This applied to those who considered themselves of the *promise* and now those of the *blessing*. There was no exclusion. *Roy* provided for everyone. After rising from his death and appearing before throngs of humans the whole world would come to know *Roy* as never before. No other member of the fifth dimension staff could have ever even considered the magnitude of *Roy's* actions.

Even while Niles fought with Roy, he realized *Roy* clearly had the advantage, stronger than before. It was the dawn of a new Yom. Niles knew he had time though; he had no plan to yield on his quest. He would do battle until the very end, until only Niles or Roy reigned *supreme*.

As his only presence on Terra, the messages Roy's offspring related in his many discussions with humans included, "Flee from all forms of sorcery. No witchcraft. Avoid the occult. Say no to fortune tellers, trances, horoscopes, séances, vampires, casting spells, astrology, and more. These will allow Niles's access into your heart and soul. Do not let him take over your life.

"Protect your home from vehicles in which the evil spirits can arrive. Cleanse and protect your dwelling place from possessions displeasing to Roy.

"Seducing evil spirits thrive in many areas to include opiates, music, gambling halls, theater, and the airwaves. Be alert to proclamations by Niles and his evil companions and the presence of such wickedness in the choices you make.

"Break the cycle of family troubles caused by Niles. Resist until the powers of Roy will set you free.

"Know this. You cannot eat and drink with Roy and at the same time eat and drink with Niles. You cannot come to Roy's table as well as Niles's table. You choose. It's your choice. It is only Roy's party that will leave you fulfilled."

The Intuits—
the Awakening

Following the horrendous death and events leading up to and subsequent to the sacrificial saving grace of Ram, Terra came to know Roy as never before. The chosen and all others were made children of Roy—men, women, Semite, pagan, or gentile. The Intuits were changed forever, left their homes and traveled to the corners of Terra sharing the message of Ram's life, death, and resurrection. It was the *awakening*. The resurrection of Ram was Roy's announcement to Terra that what was engineered here was for everyone. The pathway to DE was open.

So enraptured by the events leading up to, then the unexpected, the personal sacrifice for humans, to be followed by the even more astounding post-death activity and presence of Ram, the Intuits laid down their lives for what they now knew was true. More than witnesses they became spokespersons, representatives, living testimonies to what many would only doubt and consider impossible, even a fake.

As a band of brothers from many towns and having different professions they followed Ram and witnessed his life, his wonders, his counseling of others, his healing powers, and his humility. Some had beards, all had long hair, they dressed in tunics of various shapes and sizes, colors and stripes, wore sandals, and walked with staffs. None bore arms, weapons of any kind, except possibly a knife to cut through bramble on the roads they traveled.

Much of what they heard and learned when Ram was alive left questions and doubts. It was all so different from what they knew, from the culture in which they were raised. After his death, his appearance to them, it all became clear. They were struck with the pneuma, and the gift Ram gave became a mark on their souls as they went forth to preach and share with others the glory they knew.

In addition to the Intuits, hundreds of witnesses to Ram during his lifetime and after his death shared their stories. Records were kept and letters written to congregations of followers of Roy and Ram. Men and women joined together in honoring and loving the mercy and grace provided them by *Roy*. The *pneuma* of Roy that descended upon them and others that gathered produced a new *self*, a new purpose, and gave meaning to their lives. They listened, believed, and changed the way they lived. They loved Roy, and they loved their neighbors. They became defenders and champions of Ram. They were important characters in the *new story*. They were compelled to share so others may know and accept. There was nothing more essential than to speak with unparalleled confidence about the assurance of their salvation.

As the years passed after the tragic and purposeful death of Ram, his example was used and taught by Intuits and followers. The miraculous acts performed were recorded. The humility of the man-Roy was trumpeted so even authorities would see how a person without political stature could make a difference. Inspired words of Ram, the *words* themselves, as if Ram was here and now, were copied, translated, spoken, and shared throughout Terra. Documentation began immediately and within twenty, thirty, forty, and fifty years after Ram's demise became widespread.

Every effort was made to make others aware of the experience, relate the truth inherent in his life, actions and sayings, capturing the moments, and making available to all humans this hands-on connection to and with Roy. If it could be the same as living with Ram, which it could not, it would have been the wonder of all wonders. The best possible presentation was given in the hope that humans would believe more now than ever in Roy. His wonderful gift was intended to endure for all times.

Timely is the best word to describe what was recorded about the life and times of Ram. That was done to ensure the accuracy of events. Different writers, Intuits themselves, researchers, journalists, interviewers, and persons awakened directly by Ram wrote, confirmed, and maintained history for posterity. Each stroke of the pen, each word, each sentence, each paragraph, each sub-story was inspired by Roy. No one ever criticized the sacrifice of Ram as all those at the time knew what took place. They remained in awe and were either a direct witness with firsthand experiences, or knew a witness to the passing and the incomprehensible but real resurrection of Ram.

The greatest story ever was being shared and the ending would be a happy one. It is the story that would be told and retold in many forms.

Peace can only be achieved when hearts are changed for the loving Roy.

ooooo

There is fantasy in almost every story. It has a good beginning. All is well. Enter the villain, the mask of evil, and changes take place. Fear grips the populace. A faction of good hearts senses the urgency to deal with the problem. Fear can be more effective than the truth and has much success. The populace turns toward the evil who offers protection. Their satisfaction is short-lived, and those who then realize the truth are revealed and suppressed. The good contingent must operate in secrecy until they are ready. A leader of the good takes steps toward a new world order. Death by the evil one continues. Can good overcome evil? It is what we all desire—the happy ending. The good becomes the victorious one and is the fairest of them all. Peace proceeds from the victory of the good.

ooooo

Staring into the night, the dark clouds, and smokelike mist, suddenly, a small light is noticed. It sweeps to the left and right, comes closer, and gets larger. Then there is more than one light, then many, a gathering of the good is prepared to deal with the dark. Sacrifices are made. Lights are snuffed out, but they keep coming. There is death, but can the good overcome the evil and the death? The story continues.

We are caught in the web of intrigue with hope that all ends well. The leader of the good dressed in golden armor beneath simple peasant dress is viewed carrying his torch with a band of followers behind. He confronts the most evil of all the evil ones. The most evil is much larger than the good leader and his protective garments are more elaborate and complete. They stare at each other, good facing evil. Their weapons appear—swords. The evil one carrying many other tools of war as well.

Their swords meet with a violent clash. The battle is a lengthy and turbulent fight, the observer never certain, who has the upper hand. The reader, the viewer, is hidden from the climax when the noise is the greatest only to be followed by silence. It is finished.

The scene is in a morning light now, and the battlefield is behind a curtain of thick dust. The curtain tears from top to bottom, the dust falling to the ground to the right and the left. Difficult to distinguish but a figure, as an apparition, appears coming closer and closer, becoming clearer and clearer. It is....

The evil one proudly comes out of the dust waving his weapons of destruction. Disheveled and damaged, it is clearly not the one people wanted. The audience gasps. This is not the joyful outcome expected. When he speaks, it is in a deep rough and brusque tone.

"It is finished. I am the overlord of the cosmos. Good is dead!"

The people cower. They are lost and have lost any sense of direction.

A breeze picks up. The whir and whoosh of air moving branches of trees to and fro masks other sounds. The evil overlord has the populace kneel at his command. The wind velocity increases. Head hair is tossed and heads turned. Scarves around necks stir and slap against cheeks. Above a whirlwind forms as a spiral descending from above. The people drawn by the confusion cannot resist looking upwards.

Miraculously the shape of a face appears becoming more recognizable as in falls. It is the good-leader. He is looking down on everything and focused on the evil overlord. He has a unique aura about him. The overlord looks up in disbelief. He puts a hand over his forehead to provide a shadow from that emanation from above.

He calls out, "You are dead."

In response, "but I am *risen*, and here to protect everyone from the evil you have caused. They will be free as you will die."

"That cannot be," Evil speaks.

"But you and they can see. It is me and can be," Good answers.

The good leader alights on the surface to face the overlord. With the people witnessing, and with a swift motion of his right arm it was as if a sword of fire blazed through the center of this large evil element, his body engulfed in a vibrant, brilliant, ball of flame. It was over in an instant and all that remained of the overlord was a black dot. The sun arose in full glory to shine on the populace. It was over. The sky cleared. It was calm. The people rose and, as a chorus, cheered their freedom. The people turned to the good.

"Stay with us."

"I can no longer be with you as I am, but I will be with you as you want me to be and as I was for you and as you can be for all others," the good leader said.

Know the good will stay with you; it will dwell inside you and forever guide you from the sword of the evil overlord. He then calls for the people to collectively guide each other and live caring for, protecting and loving one another.

There is a happy ending. It is not though without toil, suffering, obedience, repentance, and love for Ram.

ooooo

The Intuits traveled individually to many areas of Terra spreading the story of the events they experienced, and the wisdom they now possessed. The *pneuma* was with them. They were embraced and attacked. They suffered often in their effort to make known what all should know and realize is their pathway to a destiny in the eternal kingdom. Open your hearts, know, understand, and believe. What took place on Terra was to convict more to the reality of Roy. They succeeded as the growth of the Ram followers was exponential. Yet there were many who denied the facts knowing how their lives would need to change to do what is right.

The Intuits entered areas where pagan practices were all that was known. That which was good was not perceived fully, and as often the case, the strong, the warlike, the despicable prevailed and in tyrannical fashion caged their populace to cower to their demands and support their preferences. Those less privileged suffered. The Intuits freed many from their plight and gave hope and joy to those who lived in desperate straits. Eyes opened to a better life.

The Intuits brought news, the news of Ram, it was good news. The reports were uplifting and joyful. Despite living in despair, many saw a new light. The story of Roy, Ram, the *pneuma*—*Roy*, was being brought to areas for the first time.

Oddly enough after many millennia there were areas of Terra that had still not heard the *story*.

ooooo

All but one of the Intuits died as a martyr serving *Roy*. They were tossed off cliffs, burned, flayed, and even killed in the same fashion as Ram. Those in denial, those that did not want to hear the truth, those whose power was threatened, those who felt they were like Roy but human, needed to rid Terra of Intuits and disciples of the Intuits telling these stories, sharing these events, and turning the people in a direction, emboldened by this truth, in collective opposition to the authority of that time and place.

"We must rid the area of this intrusion into our domain, this attempt to unseat us from our self-established thrones, demanding respect and getting it by force as, if and when needed." This was their thinking.

They saw in their reflection, facts as to who they really were which they preferred to remain unknown. New light shining on their prisoners had to be extinguished. The bearers of the torches of honesty were on the front lines and became the obvious object of the deranged methods of eradication by the autocrats, plutocrats, and councils that derived their positions and personal benefits at the expense of others.

Captured, tortured, and often ordered to bow down to the authority of the lands being visited, the Intuits would paraphrase Ram, "We shall worship Ram, our Roy, and him only shall we serve."

The Intuits suffered, yet gloried in knowing Ram and Roy as no other. They are all in DE, continuing to serve. The last Intuit wrote the conclusion to the book of Roy, a forecast, but clearly a forecast with a happy ending. Ram will return and all will be well in the New Terra.

The wonder behind the *wonder* of Terra was made known, having lived with the humans, and having provided a transformative means to correct *justice*. *The new story* continues.

The Light Shines

Civilization attained its highest standards after *Roy's* appearance, even though it was not without continued struggle. He made mankind more aware of their role toward the environment, toward one another and toward *Roy*. Liberty, hope, borne out of nothing, contingencies, happenings, drama, comedy, love, and tragedy are all a part of the freedom of *Roy's* humans. *Roy* was now seen as the combined persons of Roy, Ram, and *Roy's pneuma*. The before and after of Ram would fill the history of humans, their nature, and their future.

Through *Roy* mankind would know the gracious process for which *Roy* intended Terra and just how to be saved for *Roy's* next Terra. All of *Roy's* children would now be able to live in the light. *Roy's* children would know their A-man, E-woman, child relationship, as the composite unity of the family. Only as a family could they continue to grow the union of Terra-souls joined together as Aspen trees in knowing *Roy*. They would instruct their family and others, as best they could, in the ways of *Roy*, the teachings and instructions of *Roy*, the history of *Roy*.

Teachings would include the bad news of man's inability to contend with their fleshly existence, even as believers, especially as nonbelievers. Teachings now would include the saving grace of Roy; the substitution of Ram, now punished, making possible a seat at Roy's table in DE. Teachings would include the meaning of Roy's *pneuma*, the brilliant light of his essence relit in those that understand, know, accept, and are thankful. This is the good news.

Humans could not and cannot achieve their place in DE without *Roy*. The laws gave examples of what goodness means, but to be good would always be fraught with Niles, *the lie*. No longer would strict adherence to the laws, not even allowing for one deviation, be required. The laws would serve their purpose as humans filled with *Roy's* pneuma will comply to the extent humanly possible; their stumbles with petition forgiven, and their salvation assured.

Humans would know it would always be good to protect and allow nothing to dilute the knowledge, the ethical, and the moral standards, established by *Roy*. By doing so, they would know also that mankind would always preserve the best of relations—if studied, understood, practiced, and applied.

Many in the world would resist, however, fighting against the meaning of *Roy*.

Those most deserving of *Roy's* graciousness would have a hidden tattoo; they themselves would not be aware of its presence, but *Roy* would; it was the *pneuma*. Many would have a sense, and a condition that would give them a countenance, strength, happiness, and a peace that they had the tattoo. The *pneuma* was Roy's seal, his guarantee that they were in his camp, and would be alongside *Roy* always—as Roy is alongside everyone. Those possessed with the pneuma would be inheritors of *Roy's* glorious future. The realities of the future would be present in those so marked, so accepting of Roy's place in their nature—their person; it would become a part of them.

The process works something like this—a human proceeds in life and is met by challenges, to include temptations. Be they sexual, laziness, gluttonous, hatefulness, envy or jealousy, want, or pride, they can consume the individual. Our human example is a guitar-man. He finds working anathema. Society enables this artist musician to be indolent surviving day to day on government handouts, or the largesse of others. He phones others for free using a cell phone provided by his government. He enjoys shopping, enjoys large screen TV, and sits on a sofa eating popcorn bought with government ration-stamps.

"This is great," guitar-man proclaims.

"I would have it no other way. I can just meet with my garage band each day and play, even if we never have a hit. Tonight we are eating lobster! We can pool our food stamps and buy beer, and food to enjoy. Why work? This we deserve. There is no way I am allowing those federal legislative conservatives to take any of this away. As a citizen in this country we can enjoy what others have earned; it is what our president calls, *fairness*. And I agree, and so does my girlfriend."

Life is proceeding but there are bumps along the way. One day the power is turned off, the amplifiers do not work. No one paid the electric bill. The food in the fridge spoils; the band members are a no show; the beer is warm—why is this happening? A friend comes by and suggests they go to the nearby house of worship where there is a food kitchen.

"No way am I going to the house of worship," declares guitar-man.

"I do not believe in that stuff."

"But they have hot food. Come on, aren't you hungry?" asked his friend.

"Food. I will go for the food, okay."

Before the meal, a speaker tells them about Ram. They then pray before their meal. They are thankful.

The guitar-man returns to the prior living arrangements. Giving thought to what took place, *Those people seemed happy, especially those serving in the food line. They did not need to be there. What the speaker said about Ram, Wow!, that was powerful. He died for me. I know I am lazy and sinful, but I am now willing to admit that.*

Have I taken a leap of faith? My guitar playing; I love that. Did I do that myself, or was Roy there to help me. Yes, Roy was there. I can-

not say *I learned this. I even had the ability to learn this, on my own. Thanks be to Roy. I am a mess. I should pray.*

Dear Ram I am indebted to you for your sacrifice. I can do more with my life. I have purpose. You give me strength. I repent and thank you for the forgiveness you have so humbly provided. No friend of mine would do that for me. I am from this day forward committing my life to you Ram.

A quiet calm filled the room. Guitar-man sat silently. His heart was beating. A tear came to his eye. *What have I been doing with my life? This is a dead end. I need to praise Roy when I play. Thanks for making me the musician I am.*

Suddenly the power came back on. Light filled the space. A ray of sun fell on his guitar. He picked it up, turned on the amp, plugged in, and began to play the sweetest music that ever his instrument was capable of, so he thought. He felt a bodily change, marked with a presence that was not his own, an influence that from that day forward kept telling guitar-man "you are a child of Roy. Love him; he loves you. See a future with him and your time on Terra will have meaning."

The *pneuma* was resident in this newly born person of Roy.

ooooo

Niles was able to also recognize the tattoo, the *pneuma*, and it gave him fits. Niles was not defeated, deflated, yes, but not defeated. It had become, though, a losing battle.

Roy had put in place the mechanism for the total destruction of Niles, but Niles would continue to fight back. Niles is creative in his own right but not for the purposes of good. After *Roy's* ascension, Niles experienced the growth and strength of an army, a force in support of *Roy*. It was all inclusive. Niles was challenged to find and grow his own defense team with designs clearly on attacking Roy's people wherever they were. His people were oriented toward Niles, in concert denying even the idea of Roy. He enlisted scholars, philosophers, false prophets, lawyers, politicians, poets, teachers, professors, even men of the clergy to mount his assault. He would have as the lead dogs of his pack three, a hierarchy of three—dragons and beasts—to challenge the three that were the composite of the one—*Roy*.

Those doing battle could take many forms—a battalion able to recruit, equip, and retain troops to engage the supporters of *Roy*. Niles would have persons infiltrate the force for *Roy* and using doctrine and creed establish a hierarchy who convincingly and zealously could falsely act as direct intermediaries between man and *Roy*. Fellow humans having unyielding faith in *Roy* could be labeled heretics as their methods of love and defense for *Roy*; how they lived their lives for *Roy* were not of the standards or in accord with the interpretations of men of power, self-styled, at times, self-appointed, intermediaries who became inquisitors. Disagreements over doctrine could be used to cloud the issue of valid faith in *Roy* and lead to doubt.

Arguments against the existence of *Roy*, the promises and instructions of *Roy*, would be propagated and used to build additional battalions against those in a union with *Roy*.

Despite Niles's efforts to this day the force for *Roy* continues to grow. The front line personnel for *Roy*, members of *Roy's* army stayed true to *Roy's* word and kept their faith. When members of the leadership of *Roy's* divisions went astray, somehow the merits of his message remained strong and in fact were strengthened. There were those that preached the truth of *Roy* to their minions even while they transgressed. These men may have been used by Niles, but they were used by *Roy* as well, and their actions, their work to preserve accurately the history of the forces for good, overshadowed in many ways their selfish misdeeds. The forces of Roy are increasing throughout Terra. The speeches *Roy* made when walking Terra as the human-divine Ram have been recorded. Roy's inspiration to all mankind has been published in a book containing the essence of *Roy's* purpose for man for all posterity, to include moral and ethical standards for all to live by. It contains no deception.

Niles's human forces are growing as well, led by false prophets chosen by Niles. But it is the volunteer army of *Roy* that is proving victorious, and when given the opportunity to volunteer, without threat of harm or retribution, many members of the forces of Niles defect to the forces of *Roy*. For the forces of *Roy* their life eternal is assured.

They will know *Roy* is one with the *cosmos*. The atom, the sun, the moon, and the galaxies are but names, images, impressions and forms that are the reality that is *Roy*. Roy came to see his engineering feat through the eyes of his foal. There is no *being* other than the *being* of *Roy*; there is no reality other than the *reality* of *Roy*.

ooooo

Unfortunately Niles has an iron fist and metallic teeth. Part rust, part stainless steel, an occasional flash of light came from Niles's teeth when he attempted a smile, more a churlish grin. Defiantly he corrals those not totally loyal, especially those born into his order. He uses his dedicated and highly rewarded commanders to endanger the lives of those that might be leaning toward a different leader. Dissent is abhorrent. Converting to the force for *Roy* justified a call, *death to the apostate*. The call was to any follower of Niles, as a posting to anyone willing to commit the act requested. This way Niles brought fear into the hearts of doubters, entrapping those once committed to remain so or face the consequences.

Pockets of people that claim there is no *Roy* clearly exist. They may not see, may not hear, may be complacent, self-absorbed, prone to stumble, resistant, and hardened by their own nature. Roy will always love them and be ready should they recover from the dark corners in which they dwell. Until the *last call*, Roy will always provide the opportunity to follow him. Many remain confused. In their personal history, their family history and traditions, there may have at one time existed strong support for *Roy* and his teachings. They subliminally garner support for

Roy, feel the *pneuma* of *Roy*, his accomplishments and the ethical and moral standards he established for Terra. The sword of the *pneuma* of *Roy* will always remind and help defend against the forces of Niles. For those reluctantly trapped in commitments to Niles, the sword of *Roy* will appear in dreams as a reminder of the presence of *Roy* and the eternal guarantee and defense *Roy* provides those that believe. If only they could recall or share their dreams.

Any attempt for a physical return by any follower of Niles, even if a reluctant one, to Ram, though, will be actively, viscously and violently thwarted.

ooooo

Roy will use Ram again. He will be the advocate for mankind. Those that followed, obeyed and lived as Roy outlined—in peace, in humility, in reverence, and in service to others. He will embrace those that compete only to honor and glorify *Roy*. Ram will reign in judgment in the final days of Terra. He will be ever present at the advent and existence of a new Terra.

He will be something to all living products of Roy's engineering. He will be a *lion* to the wild animals. To the more domesticated, he will be a *calf* and to winged creatures, an *eagle*. To those of the sea, a *whale*; and to the pinnacle of Roy's work, the cause of his engineering, he will be *man*. Each will represent, respectively, strength, service, speed, fluidity, and reason. It is all of life that Ram will represent. Ram will rule over the jungle, as *king* and *judge*. He will be the Supreme Court.

It will all occur at a time to come. Ram will be as Roy decrees, the one *being* with the right, the power, and the authority to rule Terra. He will return and be in service in the future after any further opportunity for mercy and grace. The sinful rabble filling Terra will feel the full fury of Roy's wrath. It will be the *great day of Roy's wrath*. A blinding nimbus of light will enshroud Terra and with a final trumpet taps the *last call* will be heard. Roy then will no longer help those that have never heeded the caveats.

ooooo

The Intuits were instructed to spread the news. First, that all humans are sinful and can never meet Roy's standards on their own. There is good news now. Ram lived a perfect life and was made the substitute for the crimes of all. He was punished for crimes he never committed—innocent, yet declared guilty. Roy took the bad actions of man and placed them on Ram, so in his suffering and death all would be forgiven. As proof of the over-coming of the inequities of man Ram rose in pneuma. And for those that now understood, the pneuma inside them will reig-nite and be a constant reminder of the *truth*. Roy will indwell in his followers as pneuma. For humans a triad of Roy encapsulates their being for what was accomplished. From Roy forming Terra, Ram freeing humans from the shackles placed on them by Niles, and the pneuma of Roy indwelling mankind, they are the *one* as the head of the entire DE, which includes Terra. DE awaits.

Evil

Thousands of years after the removal of A-man from the verdant garden and following the presence of Ram walking the earth, about five or six hundred years, Niles saw an opportunity to create his own force for evil.

Terra by that time had grown to embrace *Roy*, and for Niles taste too many people had accepted and continued to accept *Roy* and the moral and ethical foundations he established.

Niles displeasure with Roy's achievements continued. He wanted to be the eternal overseer, the ruler, the Roy. He was a leader in his own right, but inside Roy's camp he only found a few that would follow. Fallen comrades came to his aid and wanted a part of his conquest. He tried on various occasions to find a Terra presence for his goal, a program, an ideology, a leader that would enable a commanding attack on Ram, on the unity of Roy, his terra-image, and his pneuma.

Niles knew well the history and could, as part of his plan, attempt to alter that history and develop followers that would only claim a revised history as the correction of the past. The history of *Roy* would be used, but modified to support Niles. Many of the players among Roy's faithful would be discussed, but their attributes would be modified for the benefit of Niles. Those who forecast Ram would be forecasters too, even Ram would predict, so it would be claimed, the future leader of Niles's band.

Roy compared Niles with the likes of a mongrel, self-possessed, with teeth of iron and claws of bronze, and ten horns displayed that hid an eleventh, that of Niles substitute, his own Terra future on display.

The fervent commander of Niles army-to-be would be more imposing, boastful of conquests to be made, and wage a war to defeat *Roy*. The *master* will be attacked; there will be attempts to change times past; the associates and past *leader's* stories will be revised. The future anti-*Roy* contingent will be born of a goat and capture lands over time, patient and mean, marauding and plundering, and destroying in its path all that is not for Niles.

Niles made inroads and attempts at confusion using creeds and doctrines to be incorporated into the structure of the documents of the followers of *Roy*. Then Niles found a person born in a desert area where the illegitimate son of the first leader grew up.

It was a pluralistic world that had come to worship a large black rock that had fallen from the cosmos. A structure had been constructed around the black rock in which a collection of idols was displayed—the building-of-the-rock. The idols came from stories heard, stories told, beliefs formed, tribal gods, and stories read brought to the peninsula people by travelers, tradesmen, and caravans. There was even a depiction of Ram. There were at least twelve clans each with their own dictator that coexisted in this area. Each came to see the rock as a reminder of their personal god in an annual pilgrimage. It was a pilgrimage of peace to join others in colorful unity at a bazaar and tradeshow.

The name of the person Niles identified and selected was Yamir. Yamir's family was of the sect that had responsibility for keeping the rock polished and the structure housing the rock clean. Their preferred god was the moon god—Selin, a god Yamir knew as part of his family's tradition. His parents died when he was young, and he grew up leading a mostly normal life with a relative. He even studied the history and stories of *Roy*, and his *wonders*. He learned too that his people were part of *Roy's* history; this impressed him. Living among him steadfast in their faith were those of the people-of-Roy.

Yamir was a dark skinned handsome man with jet black hair. In his midtwenties he became attracted to an older woman and married her. She was a capable businesswoman and a believer in Ram and Roy. He became a salesman in her company. He was quite successful in his marketing efforts, working diligently for many years. He became head of sales and enjoyed his leadership role and the benefits. His trade routes covered the areas and history of *Roy*. He learned about times past and the events that transpired during the life of Ram. Much had been written and his relative, wife, and close associates told the important stories of *Roy*; they wanted him to know the area's history and the people most notable in documents recording the facts. An intelligent man, he learned quickly. His knowledge and understanding grew and he saw himself as part of history, his heritage, and envisioned how he would carry forth the messages he was taught.

Niles felt Yamir was perfect to represent him on earth. It was not mankind in his image, but the kind of man he could mold in his image.

There were occasions as Yamir became older when he needed to be alone and would disappear for weeks to an isolated area— a cavern. He would rest there and enjoy locally available opiates and sleep for extended periods. During his sleep periods, he would have intense dreams, so intense they were unforgettable. He was filled with images from the history he learned, from the artifacts he had seen, and places he had visited; he wrestled with the many inputs. The dreams, unbeknownst to him, were complete with inputs from Niles and resulted in instructions to be shared with his community that criticized the multiple idols of worship in the building-of-the-rock. Niles tricked Yamir by using the persona of an associate of Roy, Gabe, as a disguise for Niles. Gabe had on past occasions provided prophetic insights into the future of Terra and the rulers of the land to dedicated believers of Roy. By using a fake identity—that of Gabe—Niles was able to insert Yamir into Roy's history. Niles corrupted the lessons of history that Yamir had learned.

Niles enabled Yamir's marriage to continue for many years until his older wife whom he loved dearly unfortunately passed away. While she was still alive, Yamir had other occasions to visit his private isolated escape locale and each time more intense dreams would fill his mind. Repeatedly was the revelation of only a single idol of respect to be embraced by the multiple tribes of his area. He envisioned swords, prophets, even Ram, and focused on one supernatural character. Yamir began telling others about his dreams and came to convince himself, a few others also, this was reality. His wife was his first convert.

Niles, building on the past formulated by *Roy*, was gradually making the alterations he needed to command a following of his own. Yamir was educated but illiterate. He had characteristics and weaknesses most useful to Niles. By age of forty, Yamir began speaking openly of his revelations, as a minister from a pulpit.

"Through his seraph Gabe, Selin has spoken to me directly. I am his messenger. He has given me words of understanding to memorize and recite. Give up your worship of many idols. There is only one, Selin. You must yield to the one true god. Revere only one. It is Selin. He has revealed his *will* to me."

His words were more disturbing and disrupting than uniting. His focus was counter to their current positions and impacted their way of life. Trade in trinkets for those traveling to the house of the rock was being hurt. The conflicting tribes rebelled against him. They resisted his overtures. His family advised him to stop. His followers were few. He felt he was being persecuted.

The persecution angle is good, thought Niles. It provided justification for belligerent reactions claiming a defense for being attacked.

"You cannot treat me as you have been doing. I bring you the words of the one god," Yamir would call out.

Yamir was not 100 percent certain of the words he spoke and felt less than confident that he was able to reflect, as most people are unable to do, his dreams. Yet his intentions were clear and his personal passion so great that he pressed onward. Niles kept reminding him. There was to be one god, Selin, a singular belief system. Even if there were those that already had a monotheistic belief, if it was not Selin, then that was to change.

Selin was new to everyone, but Niles and Yamir, until Yamir shared his dreams. Never before had anyone heard of Selin as the only god. Niles was aware that Yamir may have had doubts that were troubling to him, but he continued to fill his mind with claims that would lead to the development of an army for Niles. Confrontation had value.

In the dreams, Niles continued to use the mask of Gabe as his cover, fueled Yamir's mind with changes to the proclamations of *Roy*. Niles's surrogate was suggesting that humans had corrupted *Roy*'s statements. Yamir was provided with the corrections. Niles caused Yamir to deny Ram as being more than human, but still Yamir wanted to be like him. He chose to embrace his leadership, denying at the same time he was as Ram—one and the same— eternal and human. Yamir accepted his humanness. Yamir, though, falsely claimed to be the *pneuma*, the *counselor* that would dwell within, but rather as his own person, mortal, and defiant. Aware of Roy's story, Yamir chose to place himself in a revised story of his imagining.

Yamir, soon after his wife died, married two women, one seven years of age and one fifty years of age. His resources dwindling he saw the means to maintain his standard of living and stature. He gained recognition from the speeches he made—Niles whispering in his ear. However, after ten years or so the unpopular nature of the content and self-perceived persecution from those he verbally attacked as non-believers in Selin caused him to flee his hometown to a location many miles away. His followers were few. It was as if war had been declared on Yamir's expressed and formulated monotheistic religion; he felt strongly this was the case—war on the person and the ideology of Yamir.

Desperate and with those that had come to accept his proclamations he relocated in a northern city. There, he continued to organize his dream thoughts—Niles inputs, and, having some followers, encouraged them to work closely with him to achieve his goals. He recruited others by paying them initially as mercenaries for his cause.

Yamir found a new cave and in his drug-induced stupor was filled with continuing dream sequences. In one he enjoyed a personal life while telling his followers to obey only Selin. He became more defiant, and equipped with more revelations. His people were to live according to moral standards he would establish. The vast majority of the standards were learned from the book-of-Roy, but included, added, were conveniences, benefits, for the men that battled for Yamir. There was a focus that all life had to be directed to only Selin. It was expressed as an objective. For men, they would have complete power over women, reducing women to lesser human beings, but the men must provide for the women if they are most obedient, dutiful, acquiesce to the wishes of the man, and remain dependent. Monogamy, the unity of one man, and one woman was modified to allow men multiple wives.

In the name of Selin, Yamir encouraged his followers to effectively act as a plague upon the locals attacking wherever they desired, and keeping the spoils of their efforts—all in the name of Selin. Those attacked had the option of joining the forces of Yamir, converting, and respecting the name of Selin, or die. In this way Yamir grew a sizable force, enriched himself and his followers, and justified all by ensuring them that their actions would be rewarded by Selin as they did what they did in his name. Loyalty was demanded for those he rewarded.

In his new northern locale, Yamir became the local leader. His revelations continued, but they also became eccentric. He claimed he could communicate with the dead. He was the deliverer of Selin's messages; the truth according to Selin's revelations. Gabe remained the spokesperson for Selin. Selin was the anti-*Roy* god that Niles always needed. Yamir was malleable.

The words related from Yamir's dreams were memorized by others, special companions, who recited them repeatedly. Hearing what was inside his head, if not in concert with Yamir's own sensibilities, Yamir would make alterations more suitable to his desires. He exemplified man's selfish nature. Niles inducements were a constant attraction. Niles made Yamir the side-show. A cult for Niles grew. At times, Yamir believed himself to be Niles-possessed. He was convinced that the sayings he heard were those of Selin. He added separately to the words with personal life experiences and thoughts, as a further guide to the direct commentary in his Selin inspired dream sequences. He knew of *Roy* but now believed that Selin offered the keys to the true future. It was a choice of an eternity with *Roy* or an eternity with Selin. Because he was benefiting from his preaching, marauding, and oppressive acts against those that would not accept his new *munificent, merciful, powerful* and *omniscient* supernatural being, he continued. Those enjoying the spoils from his table also continued.

He still felt betrayed from those in his hometown and was intent upon a return visit with a cadre of warriors that would answer his claim of war against him and his god—Selin. His feelings of persecution persisted. He wanted vengeance.

When his following was large enough, he made the decision to go back to his hometown and show them they were wrong and he was right—by force if and as necessary. He prepared all this time for retribution, for the declaration of war in defense of his religion and the suffering he personally felt. He manifested his own rationale to attack others due to the rebuke he was caused to endure. He would never retreat as he did years prior.

His treasury filled with ill-gotten gains, thanks to Selin (and Niles), his military enriched, loyal and wanting more, their banner a tribute to Selin, Yamir readied his men to march into battle.

The invasion planned, Yamir assembled ten thousand to attack his hometown and the building-of-the-rock. He began by eradicating a monotheistic class of people-of-Roy that had befriended him initially when he moved, but who Yamir then accused of betraying him with tribal leaders from his hometown. He took this group who did not view Yamir on a plain with Ram or even as one who had predicted Ram's arrival, a group that never physically attacked Yamir or his men, and after separating them from their women and children, lined them up and systematically beheaded each one. Their heads fell into a prepared trench and lay there, in some cases with dead eyes open staring at their executioners.

It was the time of an annual march to visit the rock.

Travelers were protected, and thus under the cover and concept of a peaceful pilgrimage Yamir led his forces. He was prepared to kill anyone in his way that did not agree with accepting Selin as their one god, backing down only when the locals joined with him to defend his objective. His forces so large, overwhelming to the locals, they were caught in an ambush. The oath of peace ignored. The victims decided it best to give in immediately as they would surely lose. The numbers alone dictated the outcome.

Upon victory, his followers, on horseback, in celebration circled the house-of-the-rock repeatedly. Yamir then entered the building. All the idols, books, documents in the structure except for the rock itself were removed. He saw his actions administratively uniting the multiple tribes under one authority and governance, also under the name of Selin as dictated by Yamir.

The battle was the means by which Niles was able to mount a united front against *Roy*. It was now Selin vs. *Roy*. Voluntarily or not the people of Yamir's hometown and all other communities where Yamir and his armed forces entered would lay down their weapons and give up their idols, accept Selin, or be eradicated. For most it was a means of self-preservation.

oooooo

Many parallel commandments from the recorded documents which were Roy's idea were incorporated in the religion of Selin, yet the element of freedom was absent; the element of a voluntary choice was absent. The concept of a loving god was dismissed. The thought of loving your fellow man was absent. Selin only loved those who first loved him. It was to be an encapsulated and insulated following to develop, with rituals required and imposed by law such that daily reminders of Selin and Yamir would be spoken by each member.

Niles knew the only way to grow his army was by controlling them, denying them from hearing the words of *Roy*, and obfuscating the truth that *Roy* had imparted mankind. The people had to be contained. They had to be shielded from the true history and true stories of *Roy*. They had to be coerced to attack any that criticized Yamir or Selin—in whatever fashion. Any person living within the boundaries of the area where the majority were the followers of Selin were brainwashed. Put in action was a program to convince all residents that any other religion, of any sort, could not further develop. Any form of persecution would be considered a war against the messenger and Selin. There was no humor, no side comments, no cartoons allowed. Everything evolved as a continuation from the day Yamir was driven from his homeland. The power and threat of death was used to enslave men into following Yamir and his god—Selin. Until the whole world accepted the framework born of dreams and a short history on earth—that being the life of Yamir, his Selin, Niles would wage war.

Yamir, Niles, too, wanted family traditions to embrace Selin and educate in the name of Selin, incorporating the rote rituals Yamir outlined. This was to insure their life was based on Selin's *will*. To the exclusion of anything else, life was to be dictated by the *will* of Selin (as spoken by Yamir). To consider another was wrong, an error in judgment, even punishable. Born into a family under Selin, one was taught they could never leave, could never be exposed to other ways of thinking, could not doubt Selin or Yamir's programs. The same applied to those who converted. Thus, the authority of the area, as Yamir, would be dominant and strictly obeyed. This culture became the cage for Yamir's imprisoned people. There was to be no escape. It was total mind-control for Niles. The question that needed to be asked—did the people understand their fate? The plan was to prevent any reason, even the application of reason, to understand or deny Selin.

Other religions may be permitted, reluctantly, to coincide (if they already existed and persons were born therein), but if any attempt were made to grow or share their beliefs with the followers of Selin, they would be considered unclean and become target practice for Niles's growing army. It was as if Niles posted billboards on every roadway that read, "No Proselytizing Here." At the bottom in small print was noted the severe chastisement that would be imposed for any violation.

Individual desires, fed by Niles, could be satisfied when fighting in the name of Selin; ethical values seemed to play little or no role. Their cause was considered just, and thus their actions justified. Niles was pleased with the progress.

Anyone by invoking the name of Yamir and Selin could become new believers, members of the new elite.

Men, tribal leaders, sect leaders, were emboldened to enforce Yamir's code of ethics. It was a means of totalitarian domination. The leaders commanded. At their side, scholars learned in the ways and history of Yamir, taught and shared with the communities the blessings of Selin. They also expressed enmity for those opposed to the shores of Yamir's paradise—infidels. For those downtrodden and oppressed, the blessings of Selin were to satisfy. Praising Selin, the leaders led using the diary and sayings of Yamir as told by third parties hundreds of years after his passing. They were rewarded with allowances. Yamir was their guide and example. There was no one leader over all. No head of the religion having the final say in the methods of Yamir and the hope in Selin, except Yamir. Interpretative elements were diverse and often reflected the local governing body. The focus of all peoples, to live a life unharmed under such leadership, became one of fear, distrust, abuse, solitude, doubt and submission. To doubt openly was to be put to death. This is as Niles wished.

Yamir's prescription for victory went like this, "the fighting is prescribed even if you dislike it. But it is possible for you to dislike a thing which is good for you, and that you love a thing which is bad for you. But Selin knows, and you do not. Think not what you want, believe only what is written and revealed by Selin. Obey Selin. Tumult and oppression are worse than slaughter. Nor will they cease fighting you until they turn your back from your belief if they can."

This was his call of *Yeehah*.

Whenever there were victories in battle, even one to only enrich commanders, it was successful because of Selin. Battles were preceded by warriors shouting, "Selaha Selin," meaning for the glory of Selin. Niles just loved it. In his mind it was all for him.

Yamir's political power grew. He enjoyed it, as did the assigned commanders in his battalions. Yamir was held by his people, even in death, as an excellent exemplar for those whose hope was in Selin and the Final Day of Judgment. This was all very exciting to Niles.

Recognizing *Roy's* work, Yamir made changes to the many thousand year recorded history leading up to the advent of Ram. He knew he had a connection to Roy's first *leader*, in fact to the son of the maidservant. He claimed his dictated words would supersede anything prior, a correction to mistakes made in the past. His companions memorized, recited and at some point wrote down what Yamir related as Gabe instructed him while dreaming. It would be Yamir's truth, not Roy's. It was Selin's revelation and all the truth man needed.

Roy's truth was foundational allowing man's intellectual capability to be responsible for Terra, and to know Roy. Selin's truth was absolute—whether perceived of by the mind of man as good or evil.

Yamir gained confidence—he and his followers would no longer tolerate insubordination toward and ridicule of Yamir or the name of Selin. Niles's army, effectively, grew by having the sword at the throats, on the ready to cut, if the words from the mouth of the defeated were not in praise of Selin. It became as the cry of *off with their heads* from the Queen in Red, the Queen of Hearts, unless they succumbed.

"Yeehah." "Selaha Selin."

ooooo

Ram was *Roy's* physical presence on Terra and was regarded highly as a prophet for peace and mercy and through the sacrifice Ram made, which provided grace for all humans. Yamir was ruthless in war and sacrificed the lives of many. He was erratic and hostile to those who would not follow him. Ram gave his life voluntarily for the assurance of a life eternal for humans. *Roy* gained conversions by people who understood his proclamations. The followers of Yamir seldom gained conversion except through coercion or offers of untold riches. The followers of Yamir today cower in the presence of most of their autocratic leaders and live without hope, constrained, and imprisoned within the boundaries of their habitat.

Yamir knew of Ram's sacrifice, but denied it actually happened. He claimed Ram was as human as Yamir. He acknowledged a virgin birth for Ram, but Selin was able to do all things. He denied, however, Ram as Selin's son and any possible divine, DE, connection. He claimed also Ram's appearances after being dead and buried were a hoax—all this to destroy any justification or reason for anyone to follow Ram and Roy. If the *resurrection* of Ram was not real why would anyone follow? That was Yamir's logic. But they did, they grew, they continue to believe. The truth was recorded, the facts supported, and the faithful multiplied. This was frustrating to Yamir, and Niles needed increased denial.

ooooo

Yamir may have had good intentions at the onset of his campaign for a world of only one religion and one god, but Niles took advantage of his human weaknesses and turned it into his campaign to resist Roy.

There are many, even if only slightly exposed to the life, purpose, and intentions of *Roy*, who would readily join *Roy's* peaceful loving cadre of believers, leaving Yamir and Selin for the true *Roy*.

But they quake at the idea of a call for death-to-the-traitor, the apostate, should they question or deny Selin.

Niles only knew temptation, force, and control; love and hope were not in his command set. He wanted love, but could not love.

Niles now had an army that could resist the freedom that *Roy* offered mankind. He had his despot and more would be grown in the areas where the followers of Yamir dominated. Niles even inflicted the concept of allowing no book-of-Roy in the areas where Selin's believers lived. Roy's story was excluded. Niles had a goal to use those born, trained, ingrained, and coerced to infiltrate all areas of Terra possible. With patience, his core of followers would increase in numbers to become a dominant ideology, masked as a religion, of mankind. Then he will feel he has succeeded in overcoming *Roy*'s intentions. He would change the times set, and the laws set by Roy.

Niles viewed as weak the peaceful nature of *Roy* and if *Roy*'s constituents would not voluntarily take the time to learn more of *Roy*'s grace and mercy, then the enforced practice and drills, the memorization of the words of Niles, daily required prayers to Selin, the brainwashed and indoctrinated, as robots, in the name of Selin, would blanket Terra.

Niles has his army—the followers of Yamir. Their god's nomenclature was Niles spelled backward—Selin. Their army became a religion—*submissionism*.

ooooo

Niles made available and claimed, in the name of Selin, an afterlife filled with treats, including young beautiful women, riches, pleasures, and benefits which on Terra could only be imagined. The rewards were all expressed through the dreams of Yamir. All of the legalistic systems *Roy* had envisioned, for the most part, became standards to be met by the Yamir forces, an outline of what was good and not, to be compared over a lifetime to determine one's fate in the afterworld. The strictest application of the legal system was required and earthy judgments were meted on Terra with dire punishment applied to limbs.

Yamir claimed, if upon death the record showed more good than not, Selin could still decide who was accepted or denied entry to his afterworld. Niles held sway, and no matter the extent of belief in Selin, it was the decision of Niles that mattered. He always had the final say. He never yielded control. Selin would also determine the women, children, and families as a whole that might follow the men, as husbands, into the afterlife as proclaimed by Selin. Selin would never allow humans to have free will. The choices were as he willed. His authority was never to be questioned. Yamir was the example on Terra of Selin's will.

The opportunity of increased acceptance by Selin was possible when causing death to one of *Roy's* minions, or another religious sect, or a pagan, for reasons considered just, especially just was any criticism of the Yamir forces. It was irrational. The killing of a Selin nonbeliever provided afterworld credits. More credits were available when Selin nonbelievers were killed as part of a suicide mission; then the mercy of Selin would befall the follower and the gates to Selin's afterworld as created by Niles would be certain to open and a welcoming party of Niles's deceased army for Selin would lead them all to a grand ongoing celebration. *The lie* was continuing.

ooooo

Rising up on the landscape of Terra was Niles's pack; mongrels bearing their iron teeth. Yamir stood at the head, a false prophet, reciting the whispers of Niles, Niles as an apparition, an apparition mimicked from the prophets of Roy's past. Selin was their supernatural being whose name when often repeated gave Niles goose bumps of excitement. He was in love with himself—the selfie of all selfies.

Images of Selin or Yamir were suppressed, enjoined, and disallowed. The no-image demand is for concern of what the outcome would look like—unflattering, deceiving and mean—as was Niles.

The joy of his growing army pleased Niles and only encouraged him to push harder to subjugate more under his regime. His claws of bronze were ready to dig into the backs of any who turned away or turned on him. All in his view would be controlled—that was his desire.

His tendencies were imperialistic. All actions were in the name of Selin. Having no universal *submissionism* bishop or pope was by design. This was a religion for men, for cowards to use to demand respect. It was a shield to hide their totalitarian objectives. Happiness for the people was not warranted. Freedom meant uprisings. Dissent was to be thwarted. If one were to stray from the fundamentals, there would be others willing to wield their cannons and fire upon the traitors. Those having strayed would be condemned. Multiple heads assured no one head might take a more peaceful path, or even attempt to separate their religion from their governance, or modernize and adapt the religion to changes that have taken place over centuries of Terra development. They would infiltrate and in the name of Selin establish model cities and laws with the most diabolic and repressive means to punish. Growing from within a peaceful culture was another means to achieve the objectives Niles had for defeating Roy. Only adherence to the claims, life, and dictates of Yamir was permitted, with life to continue as it did when Yamir was alive.

ooooo

Niles cried out from his ethereal hole in a throaty emphysema impacted fashion to Roy, "See what I have done. See me. See me! I am gaining. I am hurting you. I will continue. Watch me succeed. Your army will be destroyed. They are complacent. I am proving myself. I am the stronger. I am Niles. See me!"

Roy observing, without words, but thoughts, "*We see. You will never stop seeing me Niles. You are my arch-enemy. My eternal kingdom only awaits my followers. Your followers, your mob, will never see the light, except for that of a vat of burning liquid flowing into the river ablaze with the flames of your demise. We will do battle until the end of the age of space, time and Terra. However, victory for those on my side is assured. I know Niles, you will always tremble at the judgment I have prepared for you.*"

Niles wanted a verbal response from Roy, recognition, an acclamation of his growing strength. It was not forthcoming. He paced.

Roy reminds his people daily, "Establish yourself with me. You will be a great distance from the oppression. You will not be afraid. No weapon ever formed to be used against you will succeed. No words of abuse or judgment shall condemn you. This is my guarantee. My *pneuma* will be as a reminder. This I say. Hold firmly to my promises until my work is completed in you.

"Niles can get to you, control you, only if you let him, or are coerced by others in his name. Stand up for your rights. If oppressed, yet with a passion for me, if that is the case, then know I am here for you. There will be suffering. Be strong with the knowledge my love for you abounds; my grace and mercy is your reward."

Between Terra and Dimension Eternal

Niles has his finger on the trigger of the human race. He has been the tempter and uncovered pockets of people easily swayed. He found the means to divert the attention of billions from the promises of Roy. That is on Terra. To Dimension Eternal, he often returns with his cadre of fallen seraphs at his side in conflict with Roy's associates, most often led by Mike. Mike's primary role is as protector of the people of Roy.

Roy's position as leader of the cosmos is a problem for Niles. He is most pleased when people view Roy's directives as meaningless. Niles says, "let them live their lives as they wish; to love and to play as they wish."

He enjoys those who speak out against Roy and cause concern, confusion and raise doubts toward the correct nature of Roy.

"Roy's plan and purposes are of no consequence," is the claim Niles would make.

In one meeting Mike, on guard, upon seeing Niles, called out, "What are you up to this time?"

Niles answered, "One of these visits, I will assume total control."

Mike replied, "You, of all *beings*, know that will never happen."

Niles, his eyes squinting, his mouth turned-up, proclaimed, "Time is on my side, I will gain more that follow me than Roy. Just watch."

Mike said, "You are the patriarch of lies and deception; you disguise yourself in devious ways and are a thorn in the side of those of the *light*. You know you cannot be victorious. The end, your end has been mapped out. Why not just give up now? Throw yourself at the mercy of Roy."

A pause, and then Mike continued, "You cannot eliminate any who seek Roy. I know you would kill them all if you could. If not, you will work at destroying what they believe. I will protect them."

"Until I am sentenced to the destiny Roy promises I will resist and fight to overturn his plan. Listen, I have attracted the *beast* and the *false prophet*. These capable humans will stimulate others to follow their course, my directives. It is already happening and it is successful," Niles stated.

"When Ram died, he suffered for all those you deceived, enticed, encouraged, convinced, and seduced with your empty pleasures and false idols. You know you were defeated. Your sentence has not been fully carried out. That is correct. But you continue to fight a losing battle. Your destiny is sealed," said Mike.

"So you say," was Niles retort.

"Why would Roy do that? What was his purpose?" Niles asked.

Mike made it clear, "To save mankind. That you know. He provided the means to overcome your embrace. They transgressed because of you. Roy found the way to forgive them. Roy also found the way for all humans, the people of Roy and everyone else, to be free of you."

Mike explained, "Ram restored man for himself, imperfections of humans cleansed, made pure, as was the DNA of Ram's virgin mother, cleansed by the divine nature of Roy. Now man can be evaluated by his love for Roy, justified in his love, and as a volunteer for the demands of Roy."

Defiant, Niles stated, "We'll see. I know my final demise will not be immediate. I have time. And I can win in DE too."

Mike, defiant, "That is just not possible. The plans have been established. You will have some time, yes, but your evil doings will be stopped. More will come to Roy, knowing him well and serving him completely."

Niles gestured to Terra, pointing, "It's working now. See my army grow. The Umanistas are growing too."

"Niles, it is useless. Why must you insist on causing such turmoil?" Mike asked.

Niles defended his position, "I am not welcome here, but on Terra I have found a home. I have followers and their numbers are growing. They may not see me as Roy, but they know me better. They enjoy what I offer them and so much more.

"Mike, give up, it is so much better with me. Come to my side. You know how many seraphs have already joined my camp of demons. They are helping me to infect mankind. You can rule along side me!"

"It can never happen. My position is secure and will always be here, with Roy, with the *truth*. You know as well as I do the future. The end will be horrific for all those that join forces with you. Why are you doing this to them?" Mike asked.

Niles answered, "Why? Why not? It is more enjoyable for them. Most have accepted when they die, they die. So live now. They fear death, yes; it is for them the end. So they live for the here and now. You know—eat, drink and be merry for tomorrow...."

"You know that is not true. Their death is not the end," Mike said.

"But, they don't. They do not accept the truth. There are too many questions It is too hard to understand and live by Roy's commands. I make it so much easier. They may know or sense the truth, but I have succeeded in convincing them otherwise. They have so much doubt. Roy is not real; and they believe that more than the facts. Besides it is too difficult for them to get to know Roy and to understand. My pathway is much simpler, and focused on the *me* inside everyone," Niles said as he lay claim to human frailties.

Then Mike said, "The book, they know the truth from the book."

Nile's comeback was, "Right, the book. They are easily confused and convinced; the book is but words. Most will never read
it. They may hear a few verses now and then, but understand?
That's not happening. They are lazy, and I cater to their comforts.
You cannot match that."

"You, Niles, know the book and know it reveals Roy and many
of his mysteries," spoke Mike.

Niles replied, "Sure, but what is revealed is to only a few, those
that stupidly want to know Roy. Then they must be committed
and actually believe. Humans, they are too selfish to do that. They
know, too, the book was written by men. Who can believe them?"

"Every word composed was inspired by Roy, you know that!"
said Mike

"I have lived with it all. I know. Yes. But they do not and they
can be deceived. Watch me," Niles said as he bared his teeth.

"You have opposed Roy and his people since you were cast out
of Roy's realm," Mike reminded Niles.

"Why wouldn't I? I am as capable as Roy. He gets all the glory.
I deserve respect as well," Niles continued in defense.

"I'll have a book, too. I will find and correct errors in Roy's.
And I will begin with Ram. He will not be Roy; he is not Roy,
and what will *be* is one thing, but what *is* is another. What is written in my book does not matter, as most will never read it or even
be able to read it. That is not what is important. What is, is having the book. It will be interpreted with my influences and wants
imparted. It will teach my people to fight infidels."

"You are something else," Mike said astounded.

"Yes, indeed, I am that," Niles said proudly, "and my book will
be precise. It will give orders to my followers. Specifics as to what
they can and must do. It will contain practices, rituals, to follow
and embrace. They will repeat mantras in my name daily, often,
and they will not be allowed to forget me. They will adhere to
strict rules, laws, many as Roy's, and be rewarded at my discretion
for what is good. Women will know their place. It will parallel
much of what history has recorded. People, most, will see the

good. That is the deception. But most will never see it that way. They will love me. I will be convincing, even compelling."

Mike's eyes grew wide. "You are a Deceiver."

Breaking into song, Niles began, "I'm the deceiver, they're the believers, Oh-Oh-yeah!!" In normal voice he said, "Yes, I am, the *best of deceivers*,"

Niles emboldened by this thought.

"My objective is worthy, though—peace," Niles said.

"Peace," Mike repeated quizzically.

"Yes, when all of Terra is for Selin there will be peace," Niles proclaimed.

"Never happen, "Mike noted with emphasis.

"There are too many self-interests to which you cater. They will not change for you—accept to the extent your deception works for them also. They will want to be appeased in their own way. Also, they will never agree among themselves. Then there are the Umanistas and the selfies," Mike said.

"It will happen," Niles simply stated.

Mike reminded Niles, "We have known each other for eternity, even longer. I know as well as you do why you were cast out. Roy made you a star. You were his number 1; the most glorious of all *beings* sans Roy himself. Why did you give that all up? And I know your intentions. I am here to protect Roy's people. I will assist, as will many others, in informing the people of Terra of your ways and your demonic team. You prowl Terra seeking the weak. I will tirelessly resist your efforts and make them strong. Roy is always in control. I, among others, am a trusted servant that will never leave his side. Ram is at his right hand always. You oppose the spread of Roy's word, his book. We will inspire humans to distribute copies and have teachers travel the land providing information and sharing the good news.

"To every corner of Terra, Roy will be known; if just in the hearts of humans. His presence will be felt, and they will all be as a candle just waiting to be lit. You use temptations, the flesh, habituates, wealth, and material things as destroyers of our communities. We will build up our communities; they are the bodies of Ram, his message ringing forth and providing strength and the armor to protect them from your attacks. They who know Roy will work for his honor and glory. You will feel their displeasure and resistance. You are a schemer. We will warn believers to avoid your schemes. They will learn and those who know Roy will resist. You cannot break their bond with Roy and DE."

"Blah, blah, blah. I have heard this before. Just keep counting. I have already broken the bond of millions and millions," said Niles.

He had a wide grin while he said, "Watch Yamir and see what he is doing. Do you know Selin as yet? He is being heralded as much as Roy. I am feeling more confident daily that I will never serve my sentence. They are not resisting. In fact, they are beginning to sing my song, 'Do your thing, do what you wanna do, do your thing. If it feels good, do it, do your thing.' It is working." Niles was in a rare form.

Mike, however, pointed out what Niles has done wrong.

He said, "But look what you have to do to have humans get behind Selin. You have cloistered, and jailed almost all the women. You have kept the poor and uneducated as they were. You do not even want women educated. You have them worship Selin to provide comfort from the depression in which you have them kept. You whip them and stir the pot of hate as a device— a cause.

"Hate Roy, hate those who love Roy, obey Selin. Fight to your death against those who love any but Selin. For others, you have them enjoy multiple pleasures—pleasures that cause illness, sickness, pain, and death, yet you continue to encourage them and give those escapes from the real Terra. You reward the authorities filled with your claims with money and deviations from the demands you place on the more common of your followers. You provide no hope; love is empty."

But Niles defended his actions and said, "I don't need the women. I need the men. They are easier to corrupt. Stronger, they can take advantage of the weaker and be an aide to my cause. And we can blame the women. They are the reason men do the bad things they do. They will love Sclin, just like Roy. Maybe Roy will save them when the time comes, because they are good, good without Roy, but they must repent.

"We need the women to make babies. I prefer the male babies, but we still need the women for more babies. As to the others, well they are useful also. They deny Roy, even if they have no Roy of any kind as their own. Their Roy is themselves, a personal, human Roy. Man-Roy, me-Roy; the human that will lead them to peace will be a man-Roy that will succeed in bringing Terra under one leader—in my name."

"In your name? You are worthless. Niles, get out of my sight." Mike was frustrated.

Niles reminded Mike, "You are going to keep seeing me. You may push me back at times, but, in the long run, I will keep growing. I'll have Terra's politicians on my side. Then see how Terra's humans think. See how they change their attitude toward Roy. The politicians will all be handing out my kind of stuff, and the people will like it. When I have the majority in any given area that has a defined government, I rule. When I have a totalitarian leader in place, I rule. Their selfishness will squash the Roy lovers; use them too, as needed, to maintain the status-quo. I am lovin' this."

Mike noted, "Those who believe in Roy will do so to the end. They will not fear death; they will not fear your evil. They know they are saved"

Niles commented, "They are more like twigs than logs—easily broken. I will break them. If they fear death, they know me. So enjoy every minute. In all deference to Roy, my victories will be many."

Mike said, "The victories you claim will be empty. When they realize the sugar you feed them never totally satisfies, but only for an instant, they must return again and again for more. They will know you are using them; they will know you lie."

Mike paused, then said, "Know this too, what you call *twigs* as individuals, when gathered as three or more, in unity, will be as oak trees, strong and standing tall to your overtures. Your attacks will be resisted."

Niles looked directly at Mike and said, "Yes, but by then many are hooked. My army of so called demons will be everywhere handing out enticements more appealing, and needed, than an unknown Roy. What I offer is tangible. Take an individual separated from the flock and they will be wrestled away from Roy. I will apply chain saws to the oaks."

Mike replied, "Self-satisfaction. Self-actualization. Selfishness. That is not the end goal, as you suggest. It is an eternal life—which only Roy offers."

Nile's smiled and said, "You have your goal. I offer mine. See which the people choose. They will watch music videos that encourage lifestyles of pleasure. A red car with four hundred horsepower will draw more attention than a symbolic gesture. Charismatic leaders will give the people what they want. The media will be my accomplice. Ram offers nothing. Well, maybe a donkey. Poverty. Door to door sales. Give it up—who wants that. They want what I make available. Give me your time and I will give you Terra and all it has to offer."

"An honest man cares," Mike shared his feeling.

"He will not give up Roy. Those who know him will never be poor. They will be rich. Roy has never had a problem with people of wealth. It is what they do with it, how they achieved, and to whom they give credit for their success. The richest and most powerful leader in history was a man of Roy. He found toil good, knowing God made it possible, and the enjoyment of drink and good times was okay, knowing you do what you do for the Lord," Mike said.

"So you say." Niles responded.

"I have many with me that are successful. They achieved and made their mark by themselves—some with my aid. But I tell them all, Gordon Gekko said it right, *greed is good*," Niles said.

"They are unhappy," Mike noted.

"They love it and are proud of it," Niles retorted.

"Niles, you are gonna have them all killed one day. Roy will do it. He is the ultimate judge. Not you. Not one of your developed leaders. Only Roy can judge," Mike said.

"Mike, I know Roy, he will always have mercy and at the last minute there is always that opportunity to, what do you all say, *repent*. We'll see if they do, but my followers probably will not. They will like what they have much, too much. They will resist; they will fight back. I will indoctrinate and teach them so much that they will be transformed into one of my legion. Their hatred will equal mine."

"There will be the suffering. There will be a point when Roy's mercy is no longer offered. We are already hearing petitions that enough is enough. Hatred is an empty, futile feeling. Roy should end it all for those that do not believe now," Mike informed Niles.

"Well. That's okay. It is all about what is happening now. Who cares about the future? I am calling on everyone to enjoy today," said Niles chiding Mike.

Mike informed Niles, "Our messengers are out to save souls. You may cause physical death, but those who believe will have a spiritual life with Roy—an eternal life, and it is assured. Your kind will be given a proper burial in a most unpleasant locale, and it too will be eternal. The abyss of fire, a pit of red glowing burning coals waits."

He continued, "Niles, you have a hardened heart. You will not change and never again will you be welcomed in DE. The same will happen to your most ardent pursuers. What Roy plans can begin tomorrow. You will know when you hear the sound of a trumpet from DE. You will hear it, but will you tell your godless cast what is about to occur? You know just how it will end. Is that what you desire?"

"Mike, I am already condemned. What do I have to lose?"

"Niles, just as your followers, it is all about you. You and your *me* generations. It will end, and it will not be pretty. Go tell your people that," Mike said.

"You are telling them for me, and they still do not listen. So…" Niles expressed himself, "Gabe is telling them. Roy himself is telling them. Ram lived with them. He was perfect. He told them. I could not get under his skin or have him digress from his perfect path. I tried. He spoke in ways those who believed would understand. You have humans that have recorded history and efforts by Roy to rid Terra of Nephilim.

"The Nephilim, they are my kind of people. I want the Nephilim to love me. It has all been explained. What Roy wants of people is not what they prefer. I understand that. They will continue to deny Roy and Ram, the whole truth that Roy expresses. I am here for those that don't get it. I am here for those that don't understand. I am here for those that do not want or care to understand. I will even convince those that think they really do understand that it is all mumbo-jumbo."

Niles looked at Mike, "So now you know—we will enjoy ourselves while you all go about your atoning, forgiving, repenting, and reforming. Maybe that seventh day of the week you all try to set aside should be Niles day. As everyone is sitting around in their community meetings, gathered, talking nonsense about Roy, the others can go play, my people, enjoy activities they want to enjoy, no obligations. This is freedom."

Niles took a breath and then turned from Mike.

They both stood in silence for what seemed an hour.

"Enough," Niles said, "I am headed back to Terra. I have another game to play."

In that instant Niles struck out at Mike with an instrument of DE, as a light wave pierced the cosmos. Mike ducked and countered with a whip of fire striking Niles and making him stumble. Their weapons were as no man would recognize. Who was who, would be the question asked, if a human had to distinguished between Mike and Niles.

The force of light emanated anew from Niles's location only to be met with an explosive counterattack. The cosmos of Terra reflected high level bolts of lightning and rumbles of thunder. It appeared figures were streaking across the skies, as jousters confronting one another. First, one would dash from left to right, stop abruptly, alter course, and move anew, followed by a strike toward Terra, then again. Clouds would flicker as light behind would be present one second and gone another. Right to left now, a bolt of fire, cracking and jumping about the visible cosmos. What transpires in the invisible sphere can only be as envisioned in an exciting captivating dream. The clouds and sky darkened. Hail fell. The exchange was felt and viewed over all of Terra.

As suddenly as it began, it ended. The two separated and were gone.

There was no Terra destruction, evidence on the ground possibly, wetness, a damaged tree, a fallen tree limb, but minimal collateral damage. News reports Terra-wide agreed with the events. The cosmos was acting up. What was going to happen next? It was disturbing to mankind.

Mike watched Niles leave; neither won nor was defeated. It was just part of the constant battle between the forces of good and evil.

Mike reported back to Roy. He had been delayed from a Terra visit of his own, along with Gabe, which he was now able to make.

ooooo

Niles had his militant army compose his book.

The dark shadow of evil often comes in the night as a reminder and to oversee the extent it controls members of those in denial of Roy. The chaotic army of Yamir exemplified Niles signature. The fight against Roy contains no border, and the odds of victory lie in the voluntary order of those following Ram vs. the pastries offered by Niles, the spoils of war, and the conscripted, constrained, and contained cadre of Niles.

Niles's forces follow as a result of tradition; his men are told such tradition cannot be altered. Born in a family for Yamir, consideration of any belief system outside the family is forbidden. Doubt as to the proclamations of Yamir is forbidden. The family born under Yamir is ingrained such that they can only remain under Yamir. The men of each family are infused with control and a need for each family member to toe the line put forth by Yamir. It is the men of the family that must punish those that fail to adhere to a strict doctrine of Yamir. They will not be shamed. It is not guilt they feel.

No independent thought allowed. The mind must be fixed and cannot be altered. What is revealed by the satanic nature of Niles and his agent Yamir, acknowledging Selin as god, is all this group needs to know. Knowledge is not necessary as only will, that of Selin is respected. No respect, then no life. As to both Yamir and Selin, any words that question the motives, the objectives, and the statements made are cause for punishment. The men and supporters of Yamir and Selin have no use for reason; all has been explained.

Just read the book spoken by Yamir using input from Selin (Niles at the controls). Born inside the borders established by Selin, Yamir and those indoctrinated into their system of reality, leaving is not possible. Unless one is willing to bear the consequences, the only escape is to do nothing and acquiesce to living standards within any micro-community all for Selin.

If one finds a system more to their liking (such as accepting Ram), more loving and joyful, any attempt to join, or to defect from Yamir, is met with derision. The escapee can be shunned, hunted down, placed on a death list and sought out for retribution. Even if a new truth is found, the fear of truth is so great anyone that discovers it must be condemned, vilified, hated, called names, and subject to elimination. This is to preserve the council of tyrannical overlords of the community of Yamir and Selin.

The words written by followers of Yamir provide the only truth the men and women of Selin need understand. It is their truth, subject to their laws and subject to punishment as they see fit and administer. Enmity toward those that proclaim a different truth must continue until there are none but Selin's foot soldiers.

The book by Niles disguises under its umbrella the composite of Yamir, Niles, Gabe, and Selin.

Yamir knew he altered Roy's inspired words and attacked the writers. They were not prophets, and thus could not speak for Selin. Yamir, a self-proclaimed prophet, saw an opportunity. He rewrote what proceeded as history and the authentic truth of Roy to accommodate his self-determination and personal desires. His deception became a buzzword of the religion of Selin and Yamir. It is right to deceive and to lie in the course of achieving the goal of a world community—all for Selin. There is justification for such acts, even though in Roy's case that would not be permitted.

Yamir denied Ram and his status. He was jealous of the numbers that congregated daily worldwide as sheep behind the shepherd Ram.

Selin too could bear a child. How could that child not be divine if an offspring of the divine. Yamir would dictate his story to his writers that way. He clouded the truth by denying and saying Ram was a fake, at least his death. Witnesses to the *risen* Ram were not considered sufficient evidence—more denial, or just ignored. He could not save anyone. Man could save himself. Man operating in the readiness of Selin's will could do all things.

By eradicating the world of those that follow Ram, Yamir, along with other non-believing groups in Selin, suggested the world could be all Selin lovers. Selin could bask in the light of knowing he forced the world to love him, his authority unquestioned, and total obedience with supplication ordained.

Niles was adroitly using Yamir and Selin for his purposes.

Yamir would be at Selin's side as a mortal commander demanding obedience just one step below Selin. The first *administrator* below Yamir would command authority one step below Yamir and two below Selin. This cycle would continue downward as a way of life under Selin. Each commander would demand total submission. Freedom was not the objective; rational consideration of any order was not the objective. Blind obedience and submission was the objective. Although alive, living persons, the army of Niles, under the leadership of Selin and Yamir and future leaders, would be as automatons, even zombies, their eyes focused, their minds erased, the sayings seen and said, repeated without error, the same, the same, the same, the same.....

To deviate would be an apostasy. It would be wrong and those in so doing would be labeled the same as any nonfollower of Yamir and Selin, enmity applied, and targets placed on their bodies so the hunters could readily identify their new prey and add to their count of game killed in the name of Selin. Heads were as trophies.

This was all in Niles book.

ooooo

It was thousands of years later, a hundred years later, or the next day. Only Roy knows. A trumpet sounded.

Discovery

Terra is neither a rose garden nor utopia. What is true, and known to be truth, *Roy* has provided. *Roy* has provided too for and when new discoveries will be made by man, as needed by man for his continued survival and benefit. Terra continues to function as *Roy* sees fit and develops for the purposes *Roy* decides.

We are familiar with electricity. Since the beginnings of Terra, electricity has been present, never visible but present. For the ancients, as man refers to the earliest years of human development, electricity was the cause of visible lightning but not known by the term. In ancient Egypt, the *thunderer of the Nile* was the appearance and effect of the electric fish which caused shocks, as did the catfish. Rubbing amber with cat's fur would attract light objects, feathers, static electricity, but then it was only a magical event. There was no practical application found for the shocks, the potential for electricity at that time.

But *Roy* equipped man, made him conscious of events that raised questions and with study, research, testing, and observation man was able to harness, even reproduce, the shocking invisible thing, and use it to benefit man. Thousands and thousands of years passed until man was able to embrace electricity as a utility. It transformed society and industry, and today is an essential tool for living. Know also though that *Roy* has always used electricity, bioelectricity, to connect man's brain to his nerves to then control his muscles, that of the animals as well. *Roy* gave man electricity for a purpose, but it was man having the consciousness *Roy* imparted in him that was able, when ready, to take that resource and make it work for all of mankind—just as *Roy* wanted.

Roy is similar to electricity, invisible yet powerful.

More discoveries will be made by man when the time is right—*Roy* will provide.

Consider if *Roy* did all this for humans, formed time and space, developed Terra, optimized its conditions to maintain its positioning in space, gave Terra its needed size, its *moon*, the *sun*, provided water, soil, plant life, oxygen, electricity, mountains, and oceans, land masses, sea life and animals, and continues to maintain Terra for man, and it all ends, what do you believe *Roy* can do for humans next? *Roy* did what he did without consideration of race, or color, for *Roy* was color-blind, and for *Roy* the only race was mankind in its entirety. Procreation was like a permit, a ticket to the cinema—the show all about the *master* and his accomplishments, just a clip of the joy and grandeur of the possible. It would demonstrate how unbiased *Roy* is, and will always remain.

Beauty in the eyes of man is not the same as the perfection *Roy* sees in everything human. He knows each person has special gifts. He provides them. It is theirs to discover, to realize, and to use. Some gifts are made more obvious than others, but nevertheless there are gifts from *Roy* in each of us. It is the gifts that allow for community, progress, continuity, and the advancement of wisdom.

Resistance to *Roy*—the combined trio (Roy, Ram, Roy's *pneuma*, which are *one*, they are the reality and essence of Roy) has remained since the advent of the death defying feat of Ram, as skeptics, including people-of-Roy that relied on their old world tattoo and never excepted what transpired. They fought the outcome, the evidence, the reality of it all.

During his visit Roy through Ram commented on resistance toward the eternal power when speaking to relatives. They wanted to travel to an area where most locals commonly gather. For Roy, it was not a good time.

"Any time for you is the right time, but it's not for me. The people of Terra do not hate you, but me; on the other hand, they hate me. Why, because I tell them the truth and tell them what they are doing wrong, and what they are doing is evil."

He was upsetting to others and needed just a little more time to get his message across. But the attitude of many people of Terra remains similar to events at the time of Roy's visit—*resistance*.

The people held back their belief, stubbornness possibly. They knew, they were informed of the future offered, and remained in the past. They were stuck. There was a lack of objectivity. If everyone were to stay stuck in the past, Terra would remain trapped in a time warp having no leadership for development and making improvements to *Roy's* place. As with the start of the *engineering* process, the forming of Terra, there was an evolving of stages, necessary steps to produce the final outcome – the cosmos of *Roy*. To that, with humans placed on Terra, the *engineering* was to continue. Man was needed to assist in that continuation. Accepting and believing in *Roy* would help considerably; everything would proceed much more smoothly.

There would be many separate religions of the No-*Roy* variety in denial of the true facts and events. There have been and will be others like Yamir. These religions will act as a *resistance* against those faithful to *Roy*. False prophets would profess their own religion, and if the only means to succeed was by force then so be it. The religion would define defiance, deny Ram as a kin to Roy, change the history of Roy's first *leader* and the counselor of Roy as *pneuma*. Alterations to history would be made to fit their own doctrine, their own legalistic system, and become their means of entrapment into a rigid, static, inflexible past. By putting forward concepts acceptable to man, with just the right amount of inducement and/or coercion, including personal rewards for the governing bodies, it might be possible to aid in resisting *Roy*. Replace *Roy* with man.

Niles will find a means to continue his battle with *Roy*, and those faithful to *Roy* growing his army and using whatever forces to succeed. By having an ideology, a religion of his own, modeled after the life-preferred by a false prophet (Yamir—fueled by Niles) who was equipped with militaristic designs to garner support and honoring Selin, Niles was emboldened. This organized ideology/religion of *submissionism* would grow and by the use of power, as necessary, succeed in having a following.

The population to grow would be imprisoned by their *ideology* and the guidelines for their religion. They would have requisite daily obligations. Many would be recruited and trained to fight for the glory of Niles and his selected false prophet—all in Selin's name. His military would often battle at the expense of their life. What would be absurd would be suicidal missions to kill nonjoiners, even those suspected of doubting the religion, or otherwise seen (whether objectively or subjectively) as persecuting any who signs on to the tenants of *submissionism*.

The same type of legalistic constraints that entrapped the people-of-*Roy* and freed them by Ram's sacrifice would quarantine Niles's contingent in a fixed belief and poison the minds of those that were on the path, more of a forced march, to a promised land only Niles would conjure up. Their life would be at risk also should they ever be brave enough to leave the cadre of the *submissionism*—Niles's Religion. Submissionism would not be a voluntary choice, but mandatory. Choose if an outsider, but once part of the program, never to leave. And no matter one's accomplishments Niles would selfishly retain the choice of who would have his promise—all in the name of Selin.

Being born into a family of *submissionists*, taught and raised by parents convinced that it was tradition—tradition from which an exit was proclaimed apostasy. There was but one choice. To leave would accept the worst fate. Absolute acceptance and obedience, without doubt, without wavering, was mandated. Niles held firm. Selin's will was revealed. This was to be taught to the children and repeated daily by the parents. Fear of the truth of Roy compelled Niles to increase his overt efforts to prevent any exposure to Roy. Noone was to read or consider the writings of those inspired by

Roy's truth. Niles knew an open door to consider Roy would cause an exodus as never before from submissionism toward the teaching of Roy. Even Umanistas, not bound in the same way, could find truth if exposed—their minds and hearts opened, and Niles grip on them weakened.

The most fundamental aspects of Sclin's religion, however, would be regressive, always focused on the period of time of the life of Yamir, entrapped in a past and not adaptable to modern concepts. The conditions for those entrapped would be chaotic. Even if there was 100 percent participation in *submissionism*, chaos and stilted economics would continue.

ooooo

Niles had other tools as well. Not a formalized religion, but an informal cadre of disbelievers, a disenfranchised structure, meant for those in denial of *Roy*. In addition to *submissionism* Niles had a separate group of humans joined by their avoidance of Roy and any consideration or concern for a life after death. This would be the Umanistas. This amalgam of unRoy-like people's attitudes would include, influenced by Niles:

- Umanistaism is being good without *Roy*.
- Umanistaism warns that they cannot afford to wait until tomorrow or until the *next life* to be good, because today— the short journey from birth to death, womb to womb—is all there is.
- Umanistaism rejects dependence on faith, the supernatural, divine texts, resurrection, reincarnation, or anything else for which they have no evidence, circumstantial or otherwise.
- Umanistas believe in life *before* death.
- The real point of Umanistaism is that *Roy* is beside the point.
- A decision to embrace Umanistaism and deny all religious beliefs is liberating

- Umanistas feel free from having to have a relationship with a being they strongly suspect has never existed and cannot be known.
- Umanistas feel free from having to submit to an authority that cannot be questioned and is capricious.
- The point of Umanistaism is not whether or not Roy exists, but whether they ought to worship, fear, or pray to Him.
- Any meaning our lives are to have must be the meaning humans create.
- Umanistas value the ability to push forward with ambition, vision, and a sense of humor when things get tough, instead of humility, resignation, and submission.
- Umanistas, to give and to help others, must begin with individual needs, and then move to others' needs, not visa versa.
- Umanistaism encompasses the best scientific, historical, literary, and philosophical thinking over that period. Science is what matters.
- Umanistaism's basic focus is different—it is about engaging with life, acknowledging the reality of aging, sickness, death, and other problems so that humans can learn to most fully appreciate the time, health, and life we have.
- The very first thing Umanistas have to do in order to be a good person is learn to look inside ourselves, understand what we love and hate, and use this information when deciding how to treat others.
- Umanistas reject the idea that any supposedly divine commandments, as they are proclaimed by human beings, ought to have absolute authority over our lives.
- Umanistas believe that laws and ethical principles must come from human reason and compassion.
- Umanistas would teach their children to 'seek the best in yourself and in others' and believe in your own ability to make a positive difference in the world.

- For an Umanista, the mourning process begins with accepting that death is real and final and that it is to be feared. Fear of death is not only normal, and not to be dismissed, it is part of the motivation Umanistas feel to live a good life now, while there is still time.

- A key insight of Umanistaism—do not make more or less of human experiences than what they are. When Umanistas feel pain, it is neither an illusion nor a sign from the heavens. It is not Roy, and it is not Niles. It is pain, sadness, and longing.

- Umanistaism embraces the morality of the secularized, urbanized, interconnected world, even with all its uncertainty.

- Umanistas accept with enthusiasm the modern proposition that all people must be free to make basic choices about the shape of their family life; whom to love, whether to have children, how to structure a family.

- Umanistas recognize that neither strength nor nurturing is in enough supply to be confined to one gender or one type of person.

- Umanista family life is built on the foundation of loving behavior—against rigidly predetermined roles for men and women.

- Feelings change, thus Umanistas feel it is not possible to feel the same way about one person for your entire life. Novelty, variety, and mystery will always be tempting.

- Umanistaism is a belief that 'human beings can get along just fine without *Roy*.'

- Umanistaism needs to acknowledge that as nonreligious people, they may not need Roy or miracles, but Umanistas are human and do need the experiential things—the heart—that religion provides: some form of ritual, culture, and community.

- Umanistas prefer to cope, making statements accepting life, and not pray to Roy.

Niles has successfully used the Umanistas, this band of brothers related to Niles by actions anti-Roy, to enact civil laws that favor their habits and attempt to slow, even prevent, the followers of Roy from educating others and leading others to the pathway to DE. Under a banner of toleration, unity, and love, Niles encourages sin and false doctrines disturbing to Roy.

Niles had a flag. A banner. Upon that banner, depicting the ideology of Niles would be a large *X*. It was hidden, in the background, but present. It was as the *X* on a poison bottle, or signs of prohibited activities such as *no smoking, no trespassing,* or *no hunting or fishing.* In this case it would be *no Roy.* And the theme, already expressed, *eat, drink and be merry for tomorrow we shall die.* Or possibly, "Thaaaat's All Folks!" Niles knew the end for any of his followers. No matter the structure of their system, their ideals and doctrine, would provide little opportunity for a life eternal. DE would be off-limits to Niles's bunch.

Submissionists will use force as they deem fit, at any time, in any fashion, unorganized, as vigilantes, surreptitious, and destructive. Call it terrorism.

Umanistas use cunning and deception, personal attacks and false claims to achieve their objective and grow in numbers. Call it politics; although all politicians are not Umanistas.

It all seems troubling to those embracing the right way to live that Niles is so effective. The battle continues. In Roy's book this battle is headed in the wrong direction, not toward peace or unification of Terra, but toward a cataclysmic maelstrom. Chaos is the direction in which Niles has humans headed. It will come to an end on the day of Roy's *wrath* on the fallen—those resistant to that which has been made known.

Roy's dedicated, obedient followers will be secure due to Roy's supreme abilities, his ascendancy, authority, and virtue. They who remain true will be held close through persevering, undying faith. They shall remain steadfast in the hope of a life in DE with Roy. The rewards of an eternal home are abundant.

Only *Roy's* faithful have an object of their faith that can provide for them a future with *Roy* and not a place in the depths of the basement of Niles's quarters. Only *Roy's* faithful would be comprised of a 100 percent volunteer corps and act for the good of mankind, loving, having hope, and dealing with any doubts without shackles binding them to another religion. *Roy's* love is unconditional. Freedom, only freedom, was without restraint for those having faith in *Roy*. They could willingly join the shields of their faith, have their minds equally educated and protected by the words of *Roy*, and with *wisdom* as faithful servants and apologists, defend their flock from anything Niles could muster. It was already known to them how death could be overcome. With faith in *Roy* a new Terra awaits. There was and remains their future.

Roy's faithful would enable explosive Terra growth, scientific discovery of every facet of *Roy's* doing, society to adapt, and people to love and hope. Fear would remain of the false prophets and religions. That would not go away. They would fight the infidels, *Roy's* faithful so labeled, as the targets of the false prophet. Forced conversions to the camps of the No-*Roy* contingent will occur. Underground worship by *Roy's* faithful if necessary will result. But once enabled to see the light of *Roy* and discover using the gifts *Roy* provided the faithful will continue to grow, and grow as volunteers, willing to die for their *engineer*.

Terra will be preserved as *Roy's* cosmic palace as the free will of mankind will continue to lead to the benefits of the freedom *Roy* made possible. The free will enjoy *Roy's* kingdom on Terra and beyond.

Know too *Roy's* self-sacrifice so humans could better defend themselves against the temptations of *Roy's* competitor, his fallen associate—Niles, and prepare themselves to be with *Roy* in an eternal place, a place pre and post space and time. It will be much better than Terra.

We must love Terra as that is what we now know, and we know too keeping up this planet is necessary for all humans.

I would want this *engineer* in my camp, and I want to be in his. He wants us to be in his camp, our inner self, the light within, to be connected to *Roy*, conscious of *Roy* and for humans to be filled with *Roy*-consciousness. Humans are filled with *Roy's* pneuma, but not all hear his voice or listen when they do. And if *Roy* could find a way to explain his *plan*, and in so many ways he already has, then, personally, I will continue to follow him and believe in what he will do for humanity next. *Roy* was, considering all else, *before* and he will be *after*, an eternal force overseeing a finite cosmos.

Humans are purposeful to Roy's plan for the cosmos.

Making the cosmos and Terra as *Roy* did only suggests *Roy* can repeat the process.

Doing it all over again would be even better—the next time. *Roy* exists in everyone of us. He was the first *engineer* and humans are now his assistant *engineers*. Humans, believers in *Roy*, whether they accept it or not, are the wonders of Terra today, continuing the work of *Roy*, guided by *Roy*. He wants to use us to achieve his purpose and as a *Roy*-conscious being our purpose as well, making them one and the same.

The battle with Niles will remain confrontational, with temptations and tragedies, but the army for *Roy* must remain calm and strong, and continue in their voluntary faithful way. Even the no-*Roy* contingent may see the problems of the *submissionism* ideology and rise up against the warriors in the name of Selin and in turn rediscover the love, peace, and freedom provided by *Roy*.

The common purpose is a Terra for *all*, with love and hope abounding, engendered by a voluntary faith in the *master*, a loving, caring *engineer* that made everything possible. Thanks be to *Roy*.

The Time Before Judgment Day

There were humans that knew Roy well. They had been imparted directions from Roy himself and also by the seraphs. These are Roy's plans for the future, the events that would transpire before the final *Day of Judgment* was made known. They shared the information with others.

At first there will be a false peace. Mankind relishes peace. Unfortunately this false peace will occur at the brink of disaster. A group will lead. An inspiring, charismatic leader will stand out. A religion of peace will surface. Claiming knowledge and understanding, controlling humanity, no need for Roy evident, people will accept a false prince of peace. It has happened on Terra before and will happen again. At the end, the scale of destruction and despair will ambush many. This period will be seen by Roy as the precursor to the Day of Final Judgment.

The complete process will encompass seven stages. When the seventh stage is attained, the process will be done; it will be the *last call.*

Those that have died in the name of *Roy* will find their reward before the announcement of potentially tragic events to follow. They will be placed in a position to help Roy, as persons in new bodies, a shipment of recruits in DE.

Stage One. Symbolic will be the arrival of a false prophet on a *white horse*. He will appear a savior of the people of Terra from mini-wars and firestorms. The rider will desire domination. He will prosper until the indignation is finished. He will show no regard for Roy, the *engineer* of Terra, or for the desires of women. He will not show regard for any god, even one that he may hide behind to raise his personal profile. He will in time provoke a bloody battle. There will be a period of peace as only a precursor of events to soon follow.

Stage Two. A warrior appears, this time a rider on a *red horse*. He will hold a sword high. The red symbolizes the blood of the wars against the politics and domination imposed on humans by a liar. The sword will be used to slay the support staff for those in control. Terra wide there will be bloody engagements and battles of extreme proportions.

Roy remains behind the scenes as director—his story and his script unfolding. The players are positioned to reveal the truth and make known that Roy's proclamations are *true*. Each step will lead to the point of his ultimate wrath.

Peace will vanish. Violence will prevail. Men killing men. Modern weaponry will wreak havoc on mankind. Holocaust will be redefined. Central to the turmoil will be the political world's president that enabled peace and then exercised selfish means to absolute command over everything. He failed to keep promises made, destroyed nations that he guaranteed safety, and more. Devastation will be pervasive. Destruction and desolation will result. It will be as if preceded by a new rider on a *black steed*.

Stage Three. Crops will die, food supplies diminish, and Terra will be devoid of needs for human survival. Universal bedlam will continue to accelerate unabated. The essentials for life will become rare and very expensive. There will be famine. Fights will break out just for basic needs. The horseman on the *black horse* will symbolize the dying of nature and humanity. The days will be dark and desperate.

Stage Four. As if on a barren hill overlooking a valley of destruction and despair another rider waits. This time on an *ashen horse*, sickly and pale, *death* personified, will he sit. Decay, stench, disease, and a dump pile of humanity below will find gravediggers at work burying the dead. Massive gouges will be made in Terra by enormous terra-moving machines. Twenty-five percent of the population of Terra will have died and be poured into such makeshift burial plots. Believers and nonbelievers will be caught in the net of death. Believers as martyrs.

Roy's truth as written is revealed, and not at all as people imagined.

Stage five. No more horsemen, but the politics of the day, the self-proclaimed savior and prince of peace, will be exposed. This stage will bridge a gap leading to Stages Six and Seven when Roy's full fury will be seen. The false politicians will still be in control, their power diminished, and their fears rising. Persecution continues. Vengeance is unleashed. Those killed by Niles forces over history, the martyrs of Roy, will be heard in prayer. They will be a sizable force to be heeded. As the horsemen of Stages One through Four represented the beginning of *Roy's wrath*, the day has now been fixed when Ram will return. A period of seven years is covered. It is the *suffering*.

The IDs of those loyal to Ram, to *Roy*, will be made known. The outwardly loyal will be separated from the inwardly loyal. False believers will have defected, retreated from Roy and moved to the political front. This will be one of the last chances for those who understand and realize Roy's reality and truth to repent.

The horrors of desolation will cause persecution to increase. The totalitarian leader, still in the company of Niles, will be scared, backed into a corner, and strike out. He will declare himself as god—as a god to be worshipped. This will occur midway through Stage Five. He will be as Caesar of the whole world. His identity will be known. Politics will be eschewed as the true nature of this political expertise will be evident. Worldwide worship of a man, as deity, motivated by greed and the power of Niles, will be problematic. The watergate of Roy's denial will be opened. The dragon, Niles—was to be worshipped through the power and position he gave the beast, the anti-Roy, anti-Ram, and political master of Terra.

For three–and–one-half years Roy's believers will live in this turmoil, under persecution and often killed. Considered blasphemous in opposition believers will become victims. The politicians will strike out against the believers and those repenting. They will tear down any signs posted that read, "Repent Now!" knowing these are not directed toward acceptance of the self-proclaimed god.

Believers will know to stay away from their homes, to hide in their fields, to find refuge in safe houses, in locations unknown to the governing parties, to be on the alert, warning one another of posses formed to seek them out and eliminate them. They will know their enemies and the necessity to avoid them. Slaughter will be on a massive scale.

The Time of Grace, when Roy's believers are commanded to forgive their enemies, is coming to an end. The souls of the martyrs will cry out to Roy. "How long, most adored and revered Roy will you refrain from judging and avenging our death, our blood, on those who remain, the sinners, the unrepentant, the nonbelievers, on Terra?"

Roy's hand will move in response to their call. Their fervent and impassioned prayers are consistent with Roy's desires and purpose.

The parallel to the events to this juncture is the pregnancy of a woman—the birth process. The pangs of birth are felt in the early stages. This is followed by a period of continued growth of the baby. The last stages can be quite tumultuous and painful, sudden and unexpected, complete with suffering and joy. The end result the birth of something original, a new creation, a life, coming unexpectedly and without warning. Everyone, however, anticipates, expecting the imminent arrival.

Stage six. A terra-quake of super strength shakes the entire planet. It causes blinding dust to rise. It was so extensive it darkened the moon in a red haze, as if ablaze in blood. All of Terra felt the movement.

The quake was followed by showers of meteoroids, comets, and asteroids dropping, as raindrops, on Terra. It was as if stars were falling from the sky. The sun was also darkened. The falling space debris sparkling as a fireworks display from as far as the eye could see.

It was often heard, "The Sky is falling!"

The crust of Terra shifted. Mountains crumbled. Explosions abound. Islands moved. Terra's surface altered. What Roy caused he could impact anew. Doomsday was upon Terra. Most would perish. It was impossible to find shelter from the storm of unknown proportions and composition. No one will be exempt from the forces from DE. It was a Terra-wide 911. Roy was the pilot of destruction.

Preachers called out; the truth was proclaimed and many now believed. It was an awakening to the reality of *Roy* for multitudes. More effective than ever, the good news proclaimed by *Roy* and believers was heard. Fear became a driving force corraling herds of repentant sinners. Altar calls were met with full audiences coming forward.

There was mindless panic. Repentance was absent. There were unbelievers who now believe and *fear*, but do not repent. Their hearts were made even harder by Roy. Attempts to burrow into Terra were met with crushing blows from falling rocks and structures. Knowing what was to come many preferred to die under the rubble than face Roy's wrath, not realizing however that was not possible. They would all come before the *great soul.*

Many of the elite ignored the warnings of impending judgment and persecuted even more those who proclaimed Roy as their supreme leader, their saving and most gracious master of the cosmos.

Volcanic eruptions began and were coupled with more quakes. Terra was ablaze.

Events—simply put—were terrifying.

Roy was acting using his tumultuous forces as executioner of the unrepentant – now many so hardened and no longer even able to repent.

The ungodly soon will be unable to evade Roy's judgment. Divine forces cannot be thwarted. The horrors preceded the coming anew of Ram. Divine judgment was to arrive forthwith. And there was another *stage* to follow.

Two groups were to survive. There were those people-of-Roy who would be protected. They would become evangelists for *Roy*. Those martyred historically, and during this time of distress, they too would be protected. Resistant to the charms of Niles they stayed true and loyal to Roy—dying in defense or naturally. There will be believers that have not died or been martyred. They will populate the preserved and the new Terra. Saved. They will be the start of the Terra kingdom that Ram will head.

Before the last stage, four seraphs were stationed at the North, South, West, and East poles of Terra and instructed to stop Terra's engines, to calm the winds and weather. They were given power over the elements of nature. This calm was used to distinguish between those right-with-Roy and the wicked; those who serve Roy and those who do not.

A fifth seraph appears whose job it was to mark those for survival with the stamp of Roy. His signet ring was used to imprint the names of Roy and Ram on their foreheads. The authentic believers will be known; their security assured. They will be preserved through the judgments to come. Once marked, this seraph will be relieved of duty.

Two outstanding preachers were called upon by Roy to travel and proclaim reality. They were exceptional in their knowledge, their discourse, and their ability to explain the cause of suffering, and this period of *suffering*. They affirmed all that was transpiring was by the hand of Roy. It was the *last call* for repentance. They confirmed facts, answered questions, and verified the truth. It was to be the last warning.

When their ministry was complete, they were called. From DE, a voice was heard, "Come up here."

It was Roy.

Upon their arrival an image seemed to come between the preachers, arms held wide, one on the back of each, embracing, in the glorious presence of Roy, the comment made, "Well done good and faithful servants."

Before the throne of Roy was a large group, those who repented during the early stages of the Great Suffering will fall prone, having responded to the word of Roy, the good news. It was a great harvest of souls, a wonderful revival, an awakening as none other. Every nation will have new believers; they will rise up with heads bowed and hands held open to DE. Countless numbers clothed in white garments will gather. Those who died as believers in the early years of Terra, those having repented, even the most recent, and those having heard the call to grace will all meet. It was a sea of white collected before the throne of judgment in praise.

They all loudly and continuously proclaimed praise for Roy. "Thanks to Roy whose grace has saved us. Thanks be to Roy."

Roy, during Terra's existence at this juncture, made much known, but mysteries remained. Faithful, devoted and inspired followers recorded Roy's history and the history of mankind. They captured the heart and mind of Roy, his authenticity, his purpose, and his plan. There were those given the gift of prophecy that opened eyes and provided clarity. The prophet's names started with the letters from A to Z. The day that is to come was forecast repeatedly. Humans, all, had sufficient time to gain wisdom and know Roy. During this pre-judgment period, the *suffering*, Roy's signals and clarion call for those in denial, to repent, were loud and clear. Thunder announced the *Day of Judgment* was approaching. People knew—they could still choose. Men and demons would be judged. Believers, the repentant, would be protected.

An overwhelming piercing noise filled the air. When the people came to grips with the sound it was more a clarion call. The seventh trumpet sounded. It was loud. It was clear.

Judgment

Silence.

Long periods of silence.

How long can you endure silence? No sound. Quiet. Your head and your ears are devoid of input.

Nothing. Not a sound.

Not even a breeze to be heard, or the sound of a fan.

No voices.

ooooo

Stage 7. It took those left on Terra by surprise. Some ventured from hidden corners. The quiet seemed like it would never end. It would last but one-half hour. It was a time of awe at what Roy was about to do. It was the *last call*.

The great cosmic war between Roy and Niles was set for a climax. It began with Niles dismissal from DE. The master of deception was to reign on Terra no longer.

There appeared seven Ontologic-seraphs with trumpets. An eighth seraph appeared with an incense container billowing smoke.

Prayers of the crowd went up to Roy.

"Dear Roy, most powerful, forgiving and understanding, come now with your compliment of wrath and destroy those without repentance. It is time to not forgive and no longer allow your enemies to continue to resist your will. It must be done. If it is your wish, we so ask it be now."

The prayers called for those unrepentant to finally have their due. They were about to be answered. The *wrath of Roy* was about to be delivered. What was to fear, what was feared, was to occur. The fear of Roy would be justified. Had they only heeded his call.

The eighth seraph suddenly dumped a container of incense he carried. He then filled the empty vessel with hot coals from the fires of DE. Those coals were then spilled, falling downward toward Terra.

The silence was interrupted with peals of thunder and Terra-quakes as the coals of fire tumbled through the atmosphere. Inhabitants of Terra had difficulty breathing.

A promise once made to never flood the earth ever again found Roy using fire instead.

Roy was about to renovate Terra and the cosmos. His judgment would bring more damage. All would be made useless. Then the restoration process would begin. Roy was about to reverse the engineering he conducted at the very beginning.

Trumpets would blare one by one. Each blast bringing fires to the forests, poisons to the waters, locusts with elements from other species, to include scorpions, blanketing the land and attacking humans. It was not just Terra that was to be renovated, but DE as well. Demons were called out and fell to Terra. The Sun and the Moon were darkened and the change in Terra's temperature made the existence of crops and escape from cold impossible.

The seventh trumpet brought with it even more unimaginable problems for any life on Terra.

ooooo

To the extent Niles, Selin, and the Umanistas succeed on Terra, they and their followers will still face the judgment of Roy. As disconnected individuals or as a community adverse to Roy, they will all, regardless of their feeling that death is all there is, face judgment. This is the reason they fear death.

They have doubts. They know the truth.

They prefer not to believe and their hearts have been hardened to the potential that Roy is who he says he is. They cannot yield to convictions other than what they have espoused during their lifetimes. Repentance for them was not possible.

The chief justice of the court of eternal rewards, in his robes white as new snow, his hair white as pure wool, sat on a throne emblazoned with the strength of truth, encircled by a moat of flaming fire. He was surrounded by millions of attendees in the courtroom full and seated. On the judge's desk will be a book, its seven locks opened, the pages revealed, and the fountain of truth bursting from it. Roy's dominion is the everlasting dominion—DE. His sovereignty will prevail.

The *leaders* and faithful toward Ram will be given Roy's kingdom as their dwelling place, everlasting, and all rulers therein will obey him, with love and hope—their eternal vindication. There will be a protecting prince, the Ontologic-seraph Mike. He will have been in the midst of humanity during the period of terror caused by Niles. These included Nile's Selin/Yamir army and the many who succumbed and simply did not accept Roy. This protector of the people-of-Roy defended them as well he could.

Those having died believing in *Roy*, knowing Ram, will be the first to be brought back in DE. Those alive, believing still, will remain, and be brought upward to meet Ram in the clouds in preparation for his taking the throne of DE. They will rejoice at having believed in *Roy*.

Those that do not believe often see themselves as scholars, as spokespersons for minorities, as devotees of human welfare, values, and dignity. Science is their truth; philosophy, their way of thinking. They are the Umanistas. The prince will protect the faithful, those who learn, understand, and gain knowledge in the truth. With wisdom life will not be meaningless. The wise will have worked to honor Roy and preserve his Terra. They will know their purpose as Roy's follower. Even those that may have died in the name of *Roy* will awaken to the glory of the everlasting life established by *Roy*.

As said, as there was a beginning, there will be an end of Terra.

As Roy began the process, he too will be the one that ends it all. He will do it to deliver those he has found worthy into his eternal world and to dwell with him. Redeemed and glorified they will be protected and free from any accusations Niles may make. They too will help Roy when he repeats the process of engineering a new Terra and a new DE. What will it be like the second time around? Is there a work-in-progress to engineer a Terra-2, a planet with similar anthropic characteristics to that of Terra?

Might it be Vale?

The council and chamber had changed little since the beginning, but added now were dragons and serpents in the council room, seated across from the flaming moat. Niles was among them—a mongrel transmogrified into a dragon. Images of the past arose in storm clouds, with thunder and flashes of lightning enlivening the trial. When asked to stand, Niles was as the dragon, the eleventh horn of the mongrel beast, and arose as from a sea of smoke filling the room. The beast was as Tamir, given life, power, and authority by Niles. They had deceived the inhabitants on Terra. In their deceit they would be accorded the sign of Niles, the stamp of deceit, the *666* address of Hades. The number was as a bar-code stamped on the forehead and hand of all the ungodly. Niles represented the Selin-istas and the Umanistas. He stood in fear, as never before, looking at the abyss readied for his incarceration. He knew this day would come.

Those found blameless would be recorded in the book laid open on the judges' bench, resting before Niles and the council. The blameless, having never taken a drink of the maddening wine served to them by Niles and his army, those who loved truth, were to be saved. Niles favorite weapon was deception; Roy's elect cannot be deceived. Their defender will be Ram. As their advocate, he will simply claim those that believe in him as free from Roy's gavel.

"Roy, these are my people for whom I have already served their sentence."

Those of Niles address will drink of the nectar of Roy's fury, a cup poured full strength with his wrath. Bowls of wrath too were prepared to be poured over Terra. They contained the grapes of the evil followers of Niles crushed into a wine flowing like blood. The contents of the bowls caused painful sores, seas of blood, nothing alive in the oceans, rivers and springs flowing as blood, and caused the sun to scorch people with fire. The throne of Niles, the black stone of worship, was covered and the area placed in darkness.

The Umanistas awakened to an unexpected reality—that of eternity and DE—never thought of as possible, always rejected and condemned as myth. They made the wrong wager. Their denial, their hearts as hard as granite, would seal their fate in a state of incomprehensible anguish. The sweets consumed from Niles's table of delights will result in flesh-eating infections for which there would be no cure. They would exist as lepers in Hades, an eternal damnation. Their fate was to be a *Roy*-less eternity of torment without relief.

All the signs, the *wonders of Terra*, ignored, caused a fate—a fate indeed worse than death.

All were destroyed that existed under the name of Niles or his appointees. After multiple Terra-quakes and violent lightning and thunder, and hundred pound hailstones falling, it ended.

Those who accepted and believed in Roy were protected, sheltered, from the onslaught Roy brought to Terra.

The dragon, the mongrel, and the beast were allowed to rule only until Roy's words were fulfilled.

The last call was followed by events on Terra that no one could survive. Rivers and oceans were as thick and red as blood. Their life given properties destroyed the fish of the waters floating on top or washing ashore. A lack of rain caused dry creek beds, failed crops, dust bowls, and parched throats, wanting yet lacking of life-giving water. Temperatures rose to levels that caused skin to bubble with little refuge offered as even the trees that could normally provide shade were withered and dying. As Roy had engineered the formation of Terra, he could well cause the destruction of his desire.

Ram will arrive on a white horse, faithful and true to his father—Roy, above the fray. The beast and the anti-Roy, Niles, had been captured. They found their punishment in the moat of fire—a fiery river of burning sulfur. His fallen comrades were killed by the sword of the faithful herd and left for birds to gorge themselves on their flesh.

Roy then brought to life those who suffered because of their testimony for Ram, having never worshipped the beast. First, it was those who suffered in the most tragic way. Then the remainder would be given the light of day, judged according to their accomplishments, all believers.

It would be the day, the dawn, of the new Terra. The temple of the new world of Terra would be founded as a city whose gates would remain open to everyone. The multiple gates, pearl covered, were each marked, and inscribed with the names of the tribes of the coveted son of Roy's first Leader. Foundational columns supporting the gates and the blessed city would have the names in bronze of those closest to Ram, the Intuits that aided in spreading his word. They were known, and commissioned by *Roy*, so all mankind, those who accepted Ram, could be thankful for their salvation.

There would be no temple itself as *Roy* would be its temple. It will exist without the need for the sun or the moon as the glory of Roy will provide the necessary light. All rivers would clear and flow with the purest of water. The tree of life, many, many, will line the boulevards and provide the medicinal needs for all, keeping them alive eternally with Roy. There will be rejoicing in the streets. All would cheer, and all would proclaim, "Hail to the new born King. Hail to the new born King. He comes in glory and to fulfill the promises made. Hail to the King."

Ram appeared with a brilliant crown, a composite of all of the mighty crowns of kings on Terra. Believers will know *Roy*, when he appears, because they will see themselves as he is; having only imagined what he would be like. Now they would know and see him in themselves. Believers will be fully adopted sons of Roy, of the cosmos, of DE, enjoying their inheritance.

May the grace of Ram be with Roy's people. May the love of Roy be with Roy's people. May the fellowship of Roy's pneuma be with Roy's people. *Roy's* door is open to all, just knock. With an open heart, just knock.

Revelation

"It is done. Unrepentant transgressors are doomed." This was the last expression from Roy. The new Terra was to become.

A chorus of all the new recruits having their place in DE is led in song by a thousand times a gross of directors. They sway in unison and their words proclaim joy. They give thanks for knowing the Truth and believing in the divine head of the cosmos. The functionaries of Roy, assembled as *Roy*, can *be* only as Roy can *be*. As promised they will be on Terra as in DE under the kingship of Ram, in paradise, having won the battle over evil. They will feast on the trees of life and endure eternally evermore.

This chorus was similar to the chorus of Ontologics that greeted the new born, Ram. Announcing and proclaiming the good news of a pathway to the eternal kingdom for all of Roy's engineering then, it was a new voice, a new song of the glory attained, the new dawn rising and a governance that insures the common good for all. Thanks be to *Roy*.

History has ended and time is no more. DE is the exclusive *club* of those who stumbled and fell, whose failings were overcome, whose repentance was sincere, and who were cleansed by the blood of Ram. Their names were written in the book of the seven seals. Having hope in *Roy* they were present to exalt the return of the new *king*. Their obedient response to the truth in their life on Terra has determined their eternal destiny. They loved Roy. They knew Roy. They had a relationship with Roy. They were born in the image of Roy and loved it!

The process was to begin anew. This time it will be different.

Today, if you hear Roy's voice do not harden your hearts. Be with him in all ways, always.

Is Vale the new Paradise? The new Terra. There will be Wonders of Vale.

Vale

A settled new Terra was formed in the aftermath of the wars and destruction.

The pagan nonbelievers were relegated to a place crawling with vermin and beasts. They resided side-by-side with those whose false gods were dominant in their lives to the extent they could not live, despite many warnings, without them. They never accepted Roy, only denied all that was reality. Niles's army remained intact, but reduced to miniature soldiers left for play. They were as battalions lined-up on a large table, a diorama of Waterloo, in fixed position, moving only when moved by the hand of a child. No battles could be won, as the war was lost, the victory secure.

The *victors* found a new home, a new existence where harmony, love, and peace were to prevail. Much was similar in nature to Terra. The cities, the transports, the homes, the production facilities, and the governing bodies remained. There were no defense contractors, no overt displays of weaponry, and no hostility. It was peace on Terra, yet the new Terra was now Vale.

What is Paradise? Was this the Eternal Kingdom? Was it DE? The labyrinths laid out had escape routes readily apparent to the mind. All was clear and understandable. Those who gained entry were humbled by the spectacle and the grandeur, yet impressed by the simplicity and ease of movement. All was not the same. It was at first a rebirth at an age similar to that of Ram when he sacrificed for all humans—a collection of young adults, alert, intelligent, engaging, and loving. They were the new settlers. The king was Ram. They would begin this new place, this Vale, glorifying Ram and enjoying the promises made for their love and obedience as a brief resident on Terra.

ooooo

Mike and Paul thus ended the history lesson they had been asked to provide.

ooooo

Is life on Terra a collection of the lives of everyone where the opportunity to engage with and have a relationship with *Roy* is as a body of believers, a collective of disciples of Ram, joined together to achieve a station in Vale? Or is Vale ever existent, DE itself. Is each life, that of the individual, the story and *wonder of Terra* itself. Can the liberation of souls be a group effort and by joining and praying together find happiness with *Roy* without the dedication of self to his cause and objective? Are the teachers that are followed assured a place in Ram's Vale, along with those who follow and proclaim the substance of their thinking and expressions; or are they together found whether worthy or not? Are they placed as a unity of souls in Vale or in that other place crawling with vermin and beasts?

The *wonder of Terra* may be the wonder of one life lived individually for Roy. Inherent in that life is the beginning, wonders, bombardments and adjustments made, a brief spell in Terra's initial paradise, exposure to *good and evil* with a resultant knowledge of right and wrong, then choices, Lessons learned, the mind expanded, benefits gained from Education, the advent of personal wisdom, consciousness of surroundings, freedom, organization and concerns, questions, and doubts.

Eternity, the future fills the logical mind, along with temptations and Niles's plate of sweet meats as diversions, adding to the choices available on Terra. In the Adult stage can the human free himself from the shackles of his past to be independently loving of Roy? Can that same adult lead others to Roy? Can they willingly speak for, speak of, and share their personal story and love for Roy?

Is Roy's engineering enough to show that what surrounds and happens daily is sufficient to prove the guiding light and hand more than human? Is an appearance by Roy on Terra convincing, or must it be denied? Knowing that Roy loves unconditionally as a parent, consider the following: A wayward child may be shunned by society, even incarcerated for wrongdoings or drug abuse, a bother or even a disappointment to the parent, but a parent still loves the child. This is as Roy loves every human. Loving in return, obedience is the role of the human. It is not a campfire kum-ba-ya for Roy. It is the heart of one person; the body, soul, and mind of one person devoted to loving Roy. Devotion is through the strength needed to study and pursue Roy. Ram opened the door to everyone and through Ram made living life for the honor and glory of Roy paramount. The Pneuma fills the person with the essence, the assurance of Roy. And no matter the magnitude of human love for Roy, Roy loves more.

How does the individual deal with *evil*? It fills Terra. It can be attractive. It is readily available, sold in stores, advertised on billboards and TV, written in books, philosophized about, contemplated in one's mind, and offered person-to-person. Roy provides himself as a means of resistance, a reminder of indwelling in each human of what to avoid, why to avoid it, and how to avoid it. But can one avoid it? Who judges? When? Will it actually happen? If not immediately then when? The individual may never be caught by society, escaping the hidden camera, but the camera to the heart and soul of man is omnipresent, and omniscient. Deny that and be part of the diorama of the army of Niles resplendent on a child's table. Roy has so much more to offer than Niles. In fact, Niles had nothing to offer but his self. Roy gave all humans gifts, plus a large carrot to lead them directly to Roy. To follow was all that was necessary.

Roy fights for humans, everyone, personally, and individually. Do individuals fight for Roy? Those that do, have they a leg up on others wanting to be accepted and not judged by Roy? Or are they persecuted. Through Discovery Terra is not perfect. Humans are subjected to unexpected accidents and natural disasters that can alter a lifestyle. Should that alter how one loves, respects, honors and glorifies Roy? That is not his desire, clearly. Is it a test? There will be suffering. Are we tested one by one, helped by witnesses, associates, reality, faith, and statements made and heard? Roy will not leave us alone to suffer without his presence to inform us that love and hope lie ahead. Patience. Fight the good fight.

Niles's army and the beasts he chooses as his leaders—do they too dwell inside each human? Along with Roy, is the battle between DE and Terra taking place in the core of each of us? Will the time before Judgment Day be when we realize we will die and suddenly declare there is more after death? Will we rise up to fight the tyranny of the traditions of false idols imposed upon us by family and society to see Roy as the one to guarantee us and lead us to our new home sooner than later? How late is too late?

If making an appeal to Roy on our death bed, will Roy believe us? You know he will know what you know; his knowledge being perfect; your recall being limited. There is no escape, only perfect judgment. If the heart is truly for Roy, acceptance achieved, and death imminent, just consider how much you will have missed. Last second salvations may or may not be possible. Roy only knows. The internal Revelation may expose what needs to be forgiven and repentance will scream out of the inner depths of your being, the trumpets blaring out multiple times with second and third chances, to avoid that *last call* and last chance for a life eternal. Will your death bed request be made after the seventh trumpet sounds?

Is Terra internal or external?

Does each individual one by one find the gates to the new Terra, Vale, open if deserving? Does Vale already exist? Is the turmoil man has described only the imagination of what might be, a prophesy of the self in a collective format? Is the book of Roy, inspired, recorded by humans, a history of mankind, destined to teach so we may learn for ourselves what our destiny can be? The answer for those having faith is 'Yes.'

After

TJ and SS smiled. TJ reached for SS's hand. She spoke, "We have been saved." Her mascara was running as tears fell.

SS reacted, "Isn't it wonderful?"

"Yes, we believed. We knew Ram. We knew Roy. We were a part of Terra. We were warriors for keeping the faith. The *hope* and joy we had through all our suffering was real!" TJ said

SS touched TJ's face, the wet smearing her hand, "We know his glory. Now we know the story. This is paradise."

"This is Vale," Mike commented.

"This is the happy ending. The good news is awesome," TJ remarked.

"You were so kind to share it with us. Thank you," TJ added.

"We are pleased to serve you," Paul said as he motioned in a *you're welcome* fashion.

"What about the others?" SS asked.

"What others?" TJ looked at SS.

"Those who are not here," SS said.

Paul spoke, "They are with Niles. Be assured; it is not a nice place."

"Is it hell?" TJ just had to ask.

Simultaneously Paul and Mike stood.

TJ and SS turned and instinctively stood as well.

"You, as well as all who are here in Vale were convicted in your love for Roy. Even though you never saw him you believed. You were blessed. Your love for Roy was demonstrated in how you lived your life on Terra." Mike nodded in affirmation as he spoke.

He bent down to straighten papers on the desk before him.

He continued, "Neither of you was perfect, but it was not perfection we sought as you were free. But it was the effort; the ethic to strive, to struggle at times, to be tested and resist; and to be an example as Ram was your example."

Raising her hand, TJ grinned and said, "Does this call for a high five?" She soon put it back down when neither Paul nor Mike seemed to understand her gesture.

SS, turning from Mike and Paul to face TJ, laughed.

Still serious, Mike said, "This is the destination you were destined for when you accepted Ram. Your hearts, both of you, were sincere. You became students reborn to the family of Roy dedicated to learning and being a friend."

"Good thing I did not die early as I would have never qualified," SS said.

Paul said, "We were patient with you. The gate you entered was through Ram. You may have never seen it, but you came to realize it was there. You changed your heart accordingly. Roy's pneuma unlocked that gate for your arrival and entry."

"We are thankful for that," SS said.

"Now go out there and enjoy every day in his grace and peace," Mike came from behind the desk.

"Mike," TJ called his name.

"Yes"

"I have a question. It may be sensitive," TJ said, being careful with her words.

"No problem," Mike assured her.

"You are an Ontologic, right?"

"Yes," he said

"But you do not appear as those described in the story. You look normal. "

"You mean that you are normal?" Mike asked.

"I guess...I think so," TJ said

Then Mike explained, "That is true. We too have gone through a transition. Those who are in Vale are as you. We have eyes to see. We can more readily relate to those saved."

"Are you suggesting there are other Vales?" SS asked.

"You two ask so many good questions," Mike said.

"The cosmos is filled with other Terra's, far, far apart. But there is one Vale. Roy is here. Ram is here. "

SS said, "So we are in DE?"

"O ye of little faith," Paul said, chuckling, "Yes, you are."

"Did Roy engineer all the other places?" a curious TJ asked.

"Of course," Mike said, confirming Roy's handiwork.

"Another question, please," SS said.

"Sure," Paul and Mike spoke simultaneously.

"What about Niles?" SS asked

ooooo

Paul provided the commentary, "Niles has been defeated. His attempt at having humans believe he was Roy, his alias Selin, was wrong. It was a cover for his deceptive practices. It was obvious his love was never unconditional. Those forced to accept grew over many centuries. The scholars and fundamentalists who allied on interpretation became a terrorist faction threatening all born into the culture he created. There were many factions, in fact, all thought they were right and fought each other. It was chaotic. Many were trapped but did not understand. Their independent thoughts were corrupted by fear.

"Niles and his army have been relegated to a pit of despair. The daily wailing and scraping of chains across the floor of the dark abyss haunt him and those who succumbed in their denial," Paul said.

Mike joined in the conversation, "There are those who were practical and rational thinkers that came to accept Ram. They showed a love for Roy, seeing Selin as Roy and used Ram's perfect example as their guide. They believed not as Yamir commanded. They are here in Vale also."

Paul continued, "In the cavern of darkness in which Niles resides, there are those who did not believe at all, whether in Roy or Selin, or anything. Terra was taken for granted. They never had respect for the work that made their life possible. Among those are some who led a good life, so they thought, but just never made the commitment necessary to become right with Roy."

He picked up a book from a nearby table and turned to place it on book shelves behind him.

"Are they also haunted by the noise?" TJ asked.

"Oh my, yes. And the dust that fills the air they take in chokes them. Their arrival was greeted by a gate opening to a path of broken promises as shards of the crystal in which they delighted on Terra. Each step they take causes crippling pain. There is a never ending suffering in their vast dungeon."

"It is hell." TJ felt she had her answer.

"What about the flames?" SS thought out loud.

Mike suggested, "Ludlow, when you leave the cathedral take the path to the left at the bottom of the steps and head in the direction of the dark clouds you will see. It will lead you to the edge of the abyss. Look to the other side. You will be able to see but for an instant. What you will see will make you even more thankful of your obedience and love for Ram. The view will last only a short time."

TJ took SS's arm to urge her to leave.

ooooo

Back in the bright outdoors TJ and SS followed the suggested path. The clouds they observed were black and just hung in one location. As they came closer, the light of the day diminished. They saw an edge, the border of a grand crevasse, and soon they were in view of the opposite side. It was a scene of destruction and desolation, as if fire, the embers still smoldering, mudslides, and tornadoes collided together to rid the surface of any life. But what they saw lasted for an instant as if a new slide appeared in the show.

They faced each other and hugged. At that very moment, a figure stood near. In a white robe, hands turned upward at waist level, long hair and with a beard well groomed was man. TJ gasped. SS spoke, "Ram!"

"You are my children. It is a joy to have you here with your friends and my friends. We call them all friends. Join me as we return to the city," Ram said.

The three walked side by side, seeing only a display of brilliant color in a perfect garden before them.

Thanks be to Roy.

If You Were Roy

If you were *Roy* and did all this for humans, wouldn't you want the opportunity to spend face time with the people, plant yourself in the presence of humans and live their life, to see first hand your extensive product, and to guide them to the future you have guaranteed? You might then decide, as did *Roy*, on needed steps to ensure the future of *man*, even write a book about it, suggesting to humans what they need to do to remain in your company, even to become part of *Roy* and *Roy* a part of you. Would that be a book worth reading? Would this be any different if *Roy* was God? Niles was the devil? And the book was—well, you know.

As a result of creation, God has provided a pathway for human understanding of the cosmos. The cosmos is where God lives, and lives with the humans he created in his image for his purpose. Creation is an ongoing activity, with each birth, with each new scientific discovery, and with each artifact humans invent to make life better here on earth (our Terra), creation continues. New truths are revealed divinely. It is an evolutionary process in which God's hand is in control of each step. As needed and when the time is right new elements will be provided—by God.

Through the Word of God, the Bible, God reveals himself to mankind. The Bible contains the most succinct and comprehensive outline for the moral and ethical values all people should adhere to and insure are instilled in their offspring. It describes humanity and humanness—love, kindness, humility, peace, self-control, goodness, gentleness, faithfulness, patience, and joy. It is the oldest recorded history book covering a period of four thousand five hundred years, or billions (when 'yom' is considered). This is a document that when you read, study, receive interpretations from qualified teachers, reread, gain in its knowledge and wisdom, grows on you and becomes an inspiring (as well as inspired) reference for all you do. As you develop in the Word, as from a baby, then child through puberty, a teenager and then an adult, you become more capable in sharing the Word with others. The responsibility as teacher is great.

As a farmer, one needs to know his craft to properly tend the land and produce the most abundant and satisfying crops.

Birth and rebirth suggest the same needs, a need to grow, to crawl, then stand, then walk, then run, along with learn, understand, comprehend, and share. We need capable parenting along the way—good teachers and guidance counselors. If one is reborn later in life they accept their new person, their new faith and from that beginning ready themselves to dig deeply into the Word of God with a welcoming heart and open mind, grow in their belief, their fellowship, their wisdom, and their relationship with God. At that time, good parenting is also necessary—trusted teachers and counselors.

God calls out to everyone, and those who hear him respond, choose the path and take the journey that will bring them to a place prepared in advance for them. It is a joyous trip, not without obstacles, but with a proper focus and continued involvement with the Word, even we, imperfect humans, will find salvation with God. He made that so. He provided his *son* to die for man, to take upon himself the sins of man, the transgressions, and provide forgiveness. Those that atone for the ways they follow led by their own Niles, the devil in disguise, find a faith in Christ alone and receive the tattoo, the Holy Spirit, as their assurance of a life eternal with the Trinity.

Justified by our faith, we find forgiveness and take actions pleasing to the Lord. We discover through the Spirit a greater

understanding of our temporal earthly existence and the reserva-
tions made for a future of incomprehensible glory.

When it is all revealed it will conclude, "The Grace of the
Lord Jesus be with God's people. Amen."

Postscript

I must thank Hugh Ross for his writing and his insight. Even though I have never met or spoken with this man, although I have visited his website, he is the inspiration for this piece; primarily from a read of his book *More Than A Theory*. Much more the scientific mind than me, I apologize upfront to Ross and the scientific community as a whole for any errors in my descriptions. Also John Walton, his book *The New World of Genesis One* influenced my understanding of God's purpose for each stage of the process to create a functioning cosmos for God to take up residence.

My objective is to share a truth as a short story allegory providing a thought provoking approach to creation and the reality of God. Presenting the biblical story in a provocative fashion, taking some liberties with interpretation and modernizing to a limited extent, my desire for the reader to want to, if not already the case, engage his appetite for literature by reading the Bible in its entirety.

Others also provided inspiration for this piece to include Michael Novak and his book, *No One Sees God*, Simon Singh in his book, *Big Bang—The Origin of the Universe*, Roy Abraham Varghese, *The Wonder of the World*, and *The Truth Project* by Focus on the Family with Del Tackett as classroom leader. I would be remiss if I did not mention Owen Gingerich, Professor of Astronomy and the History of Science, Emeritus, Harvard, his book, *God's Universe*, his love for God, his scientific clarity and his personal objectivity.

From my book *The Damascus Quran*, Pogg is the author of *The Wonder of Terra*. Consideration given to this writing inspired the prior book. An exploratory mind in the arena of biblical fact which involve events, people and geography as well as the forecast of the future was my inspiration. If there was a Pogg he would have done a much more adequate job in writing this book. My apologies to Pogg but my thanks also.

There are many writing today, I wish I could mention them all, that are committed Christians and make every effort to capture the hearts and minds of others for God. Bless every one of them and I thank them and encourage them to continue.

Unfortunately there are those that simply deny God. As stated in Romans 1:20, "*Since the creation of the world God's invisible qualities – his eternal power and divine nature – have been clearly seen, being understood from what has been made, so that men are without excuse,*" which then goes on to say (Romans 1:21), "*although they knew God, they neither glorified him as God nor gave thanks to him, but their thinking became futile and their foolish hearts darkened.*"

This is a book of fiction; however the theme reflects biblical history. For the literalists the seven days are traded for a metaphor for God's time which allows for the construction of this story from the big bang theory and the discovery and understanding of DNA. With man's presence on earth, his mind engaged, much more has transpired. The work of intelligence is present in the creation and the model for man. There is no challenge herein of the inerrancy of the Bible. This is another battle between good and evil written, however, with many biblical parallels.

Today there are scientific proofs, astrological, and biological, such that metaphysics (of or relating to the transcendent or to a reality beyond what is perceptible to the senses), the supernatural, must be a consideration in conclusions drawn when research cannot find answers using natural law. Divine law, that which made the natural and physical laws of the universe possible, cannot be ignored.

Evolution has its place, but it must be presented as a hypothesis; for as a theory, it has not been proven, especially not on a macro level. Evolution today is an unfinished theory according to many scientists; it is incomplete. We must be honest in presenting such concepts, especially Darwinism, as what is tantamount to a religious belief. The evidence itself must be the foundation, with objective understanding, of the reality of the world in which we dwell.

The big bang and DNA evidence are compelling and suggest modern scientific discoveries have become revelations in being aware and knowing God. Certainly the discovery of DNA, with its similarities to the depictions of the Tree of Life in ancient artistry, and its mathematical complexity and the improbability evolution could have yielded such an infinitely complex formula in the billions of years since the beginning of the universe, is eye-opening. Laminin with its cross shaped appearance throughout the body is another marker with a unique shape. Laminin is a family of proteins essential to the structural characteristics of every tissue of the body. Then too looking through the Hubble telescope and seeing in the visible distance and with modern scientific instruments many beautiful elements of the cosmos and the beginning of time and space, knowing also we exist in an expanding universe than may one day slow its rate of growth, stop or even begin to cool, like a cup of tea; it is heated and then as it sits it cools. But then again maybe the universe and all the galaxies will simply continue to expand forever. That too may happen.

God knows what will happen, and we should not fear, for if in God's mind we are a part of his purpose, we will accept the outcome knowing what comes next. Simon Singh describes the big bang as, "an elegant explanation of everything we see in the night sky....the consequence of an insatiable curiosity, a fabulous imagination, acute observation and ruthless logic."

He also discusses detection of the fossil evidence, "CMB radiation" (cosmic microwave background), which is the "echo" proof "that the big bang really happened."

Hugh Ross states "In other disciplines, scientists infer the past. In astronomy, they directly see and measure it."

Through astronomy we see the CMG radiation, the proof of the beginning of time and space.

And today we have news of the God-particle.

The story considers God's relationship with his creation. That relationship has been spelled out and documented in the history of antiquity presented in the Bible. This one book contains information, guidelines and facts that were true in the past and remain true today. It is amazing by its content and truth. Libraries have grown from the study, explanation, debate, contradiction, archeological proof, and gravity of the content of this one document. It remains capable of standing alone as a source of infinite wisdom.

My wife, Dee, provides me useful sensitive analogies for the relationship Christians seek with the Trinity. She walks with God in a way that I can only pray someday will be a similar path that I take. I wander (that is *wander*, not *wonder*, but I wonder, too, have doubts just like everyone else) as do all Christians, but I am making the effort to keep my eye on the goal, the purpose and opportunity God has set out before us.

Staying on the right path, choosing the correct fork in the road, returning to the way to the celestial city is essential. The *Bible* is my foundation for any of the works I commit to, in part as a resource, but more so as a guide and reason for taking the time to share the gospel with others in new ways. The evidence we have before us makes God's gift to us all that much more precious. What I do is for the honor and glory of God. Each day I rejoice in having access to the Word and to writers that inspire and share their understanding of their faith; also I rejoice in the freedom to read every line written. I rejoice also in the scientific inquiries where minds are open and receptive to a divine influence on possible outcomes, even though natural laws represent boundaries within which discoveries are desired.

May everyone enjoy the liberty to read, absorb, understand, and explore their doubts so they can establish their own knowledge and understanding of the Lord. God wants us to be aware and conscious of him in such a way that we become a part of his consciousness and our consciousness is God-like. He wants man to understand everything possible about the universe he made for man. Much will be accomplished in his time, but in our time too. It is a blessing to be able to freely share my own moments of clarity and excitement. Blessed is the man who trusts in him.

About the Author

Thomas W. Balderston is a lay writer of religious books, oriented to foundational elements in believing and having faith in Jesus Christ, understanding the Trinity, knowing we exist for a reason and have a purpose. Everyone is encouraged to develop a relationship with the Lord which can be had through the revealed presence of the Trinity in the Holy Bible. This is his fourth book, the others, *Wake Up! Wake Up! – The Testimony of a Layman, The Proven God, and the Damascus Quran.* He actively blogs at www.understandislam.com and has for some time focused on the subject: Understanding Islam. His websites are www.tombalderston.com and tombalderston.tateauthor.com. E-mails can be sent via the website or by comments made at the blog posting Internet sites.